'Everything seemed to flow in slow-motion. She moved with alarming speed. She watched herself as she lurched forward and pushed Charles over the parapet. He tumbled like a rag doll into the swift and muddy waters of the Thames, screaming soundlessly, as dark as a butterfly, as heavy as a feather.'

Ivor M Bundell

Ivor is a musician, an award-winning songwriter, a poet and a novelist. This is his second novel.

This book is dedicated to my good friends, Neville & Jane.

"I would like to thank my brother Kevan for his timely conscientious editing, and his sensible advice. Without his help I would undoubtedly have made more errors in my ornithological descriptions. I would also like to thank my early-readers: Peter Doggett, Sarah Jones, and Neil Pritchard, for their unfailing endurance and encouragement. I could not have asked for a better group of willing guinea pigs. A special mention must go to Nina Abbott-Barish, my very excellent proof-reader. I dedicate the preceding hyphen to her. Finally, I would like to thank the Filament Publishing Team for all their hard work in preparing my book for the world, if not the world for my book."

Fractal

An Inspector Erasmus Mystery

Published by
Filament Publishing Ltd.
16 Croydon Road, Beddington, Croydon, Surrey, CR0 4PA, United
Kingdom. Telephone +44 (0)20 8688 2598
www.filamentpublishing.com
info@filamentpublishing.com

© 2019 Ivor M Bundell

ISBN 978-1-912635-75-7
Printed by 4edge Ltd.

Contents

1. Murder

It is dark. The streets are damp and empty but it has stopped raining.
A man is walking briskly back to his hotel. Even in this small provincial
town it is best to be careful. He has travelled enough to know when to
be seen and when to lie low, when to be on his guard and when to relax.
Now he is alert and every step is deliberate and every breath is measured.
He is economic with his effort and uses no more energy than is necessary.
He watches a cat slink across the street and disappear over a garden wall.
A fox spies him, then disregards him and slopes off on its rounds. The late
night bus, with no one but the driver on board, splashes back to the
depot. He slips into the shadows and watches it pass.

He reaches the hotel and the porter greets him with a silent nod,
handing him his key card. He takes the stairs, two at a time, to the second
floor. He reaches the end of the corridor and slips the key-card into
the reader to open the door to his room. The light does not come on
automatically. He closes the door behind him and searches for the
card holder somewhere on the wall nearby and slots in the key-card.
He catches the faint whiff of cigarette tobacco mixed with something else.
Then she turns on the bedside lamp.

She is waiting for him. She is naked beneath the sheets. He moves
swiftly towards her. She pulls him down onto the bed.

"Did anyone see you arrive?" he asks.

"Of course not!" she replies.

And later no one would see her leave.

Even he would not see her leave, though his eyes would be wide open.

2. The Day Begins

Toby Butterdale burst into the office, looking for all the world as if he had just seen a ghost – he was pale as a freshly laundered sheet, only not so well ironed.

"What is it?" asked Inspector Erasmus, "something up?"

Butterdale was still catching his breath.

"Not a rat in the basement then?"

"No, not at all", replied Butterdale. "Not a rat. A body, a human body!"

"What? Here in the basement?"

"No, not here. In the Metropole Hotel. A guest's been murdered"

"Oh, a murder. Any idea yet who it is?" asked Erasmus.

"Yes sir, apparently it's one of the engineers from the fracking operation over at Mournley Woods. He was staying at the hotel. The maid found him this morning."

～

The corpse was sprawled across the floor and a piece of flex protruded from under the neck. There was a faint smell of singed hair and another odour not obviously identifiable, but otherwise nothing detectable on the olfactory front. The man's chin was smeared with what appeared to be oil, and his hands were tied together. His eyes were wide open, chalky-glazed and staring into space with a surprised expression. Even as he took all this in, Erasmus saw that this was not why Butterdale had been so uncharacteristically agitated. The victim had a goatee beard, shaven head, and browned and weathered arms with more than a passing similarity to the boss. Only the height and age were clearly different: the victim was both taller and perhaps ten years younger.

"Oh, I see", said Erasmus, matter of factly.

He turned to Butterdale and asked him to replay the scene:

"Signs of a struggle but no sign of forced entry; wallet present and still containing fifty pounds in cash, together with three credit cards and an Oyster card. A driving licence. House keys on the bedside table. Laptop computer and smartphone on the desk, both charging."

"Anything else?"

"Not that I can see."

"What *can't* you see?"

Butterdale looked more carefully – for an instant he was a boy scout again, playing Kim's Game. He was trying to remember what he had seen, except this time he was trying to "see" what he had not seen, what was missing, what was incongruous and might be an important clue.

"Ah! There are no car keys, no fob, and none were found in his pockets. But he must have arrived by car. It's a thirty-minute drive from the fracking site."

"Yes. Most probably. Still, better not jump to conclusions. Check with the concierge; our man may have used a taxi. And possession of a driving licence need not indicate ownership of a car. Check it out with DVLA."

Thus did Inspector Erasmus nurture his lieutenant's natural ability and guide it carefully, with an outwardly dispassionate interest and an occasional twinge of pride. Butterdale's predecessor, Wetherton, had gone up to the Met. He too was certain to make good, assuming he negotiated the political minefields en route – something Erasmus himself had never quite managed to achieve. He was too transparent, too scrupulous, and too non-conformist to be able to abide by others' rules or play their adversarial games. For him the only game he played was with the unknown killer, and that was a game he took very seriously indeed.

SOCO had finished their forensic examination. Butterdale informed the Inspector that the clear up team had arrived to remove the body, and was it okay to do so? Erasmus nodded.

3. Sam's Success

After a number of abortive attempts at youthful commitment and expression, Sam felt he had really found his place this time. He had become an eco-warrior. He had been drawn into the cause by a brown eyed, dark-haired, charismatic girl, a few years older than himself – and completely unattainable. Not that he had a low opinion of himself, but he was realistic about his chances.

The fracking survey had begun last week in Mournley Wood and the SSSI status of the land had been legally and literally trampled on by Council and mining engineers alike. It was time for action. Tonight was the night. An act of sabotage. He would put sugar in their fuel tanks. That would stop the drilling – for a while at least. No one else knew about his plan, but when she learnt of it, Treena would approve, he was sure. It was nearly dark now and he slipped quietly out the back door.

∼

As he approached the fence he thought he saw a figure over to his right, near the workmen's hut. He held his breath, but there was no one. He continued on his secret mission.

∼

"Sam, is that you?"

"Yes mum."

"You're a bit early, aren't you?"

"They let us go early today."

"Dinner won't be ready for another hour."

Erasmus put his briefcase down, took off his shoes, fetched his slippers from the cupboard under the stairs, and hung his coat on the coat stand. Then he settled into his well-worn armchair, in the corner of the living room. He closed his eyes and touched his fingertips together in a moment's meditation. He breathed gently, rhythmically, and slowed down the pace of the day into a consciousness of his limbs, and his muscles, and the un-creasing furrows on his brow, and the tension releasing across his shoulders. Soon it was time for dinner.

There was no talk about work. Julian remarked on the fish and Jennifer mentioned her visit to her sister's. And then, as an afterthought, mentioned her own appearance on the local news.

"Ah yes, I sent Butterdale up to the camp today to find out what he could about our guests."

"Well, I overheard them on the bus and they were very sure they would manage to stop the fracking."

"It seems ironic that this discovery of a new fossil fuel resource could put back, by a hundred years at least, all the efforts to look after the planet for our children and our children's children."

Jennifer nodded her agreement as she savoured the fish. She must get the tyre mended on her bicycle, then she could go and visit the camp for herself. More material for her writing.

Erasmus went into the living room to study his collection of small wooden boxes and other handcrafted objects. He liked to study the colour of the different woods, especially those with inlaid patterns. He had never meant to start a collection of treen but a favourite great-aunt had set him off on this path many years ago. He had eventually inherited several valuable pieces from her. Soon he was totally absorbed in his curious hobby, as still as a tree, as if lost in a meditation.

Jennifer got ready for her trip up to town the next day to see her friend Harriet. They usually arranged to meet on a Wednesday afternoon at least once a month.

6. Tete a Tete

Jennifer stopped reading and turned to Harriet. "What do you think so far?" She asked. Harriet looked up and smiled.

"Well, you haven't quite finished the last chapter, I'd say – it needs a bit more polishing - but we can discuss things as they stand, if you like."

Harriet was a useful sounding board; she neither pulled her punches nor held back praise where she felt it was due. If she particularly liked an image, a scene, a piece of dialogue, then she would say so, but her punches carried some weight and could not be easily dodged.

"This looks like a Middle England sort of affair, with a nod to contemporary issues and the typically quirky detective who is assigned to discover not only a murder, but also reveals the finely tuned workings of his own moral compass, at one and the same time. So far so good, but it is fairly predictable so far. And you tell me you seem to have cast around several red herrings to date, with more to follow, I suspect? You say there remains another key contemporary concern to weave into the plot somehow – no, that was included in the last chapter – but I am worried about thematic indigestion! Don't you perhaps have too many disparate threads running through?

The genre is recognisable and you have developed an interesting main character, hinting at psychological depths. He has a deputy, a second-in-command who seems a bit green, I'd say. Then there is the young man, the eco-warrior – what's his name? Fairly stock stuff I think, but I'll suspend judgement on that character for the time being, just till I see where the plot leads."

This was useful. It enabled Jennifer to take stock and regroup her imagination as it sought to explore, control, create, recreate – and so emerge into the light of day with no precise or premeditated plan of any discernible kind. She too was curious to know where things might lead. So far we had a detective investigating a murder and some other related characters. That was all. Each character seemed to inhabit their own space. There are hints of depth – some showing on the surface, others obviously yet to be plumbed. Jennifer felt well set if not yet entirely convinced. The niggling problem, as always, was that the plot may not be sufficiently interesting to warrant writing to completion.

The conversation turned to other matters: shared memories of earlier times, of exploits and adventures, of those they had known and those now gone. It was the usual stuff of conversation between people whose lives are now past halfway and still wonder how they will make their mark. Familiar existential questions persist and dissatisfactions rise to the surface again; it is nothing new.

Eventually Harriet rose to go and they arranged to meet later in the year when she would be holidaying in Tuscany, not far from Lucca, where she had a holiday villa. Jennifer had been to Tuscany before but then only to Florence, where she had done her duty as a tourist and visited the Uffizi, seen Michaelangelo's David, walked across the Ponte Vecchio, etc. She was now keen to explore further the culture and history of the region. Lucca would be more off the beaten track and less touristy.

Jennifer could not sleep that night and instead returned to the text she was constructing. And as she moved towards it, in turn it began to inhabit her, to control – even to possess her. Eventually she did fall asleep and woke again only when it grew cold in the hours before dawn, when she stumbled off to bed, dropping cigarette ash on the carpet. By then she had completed the previously unfinished chapter.

7. The Investigation

The pathologist's report was on his desk early on Thursday afternoon and Erasmus picked it up to read even before he had removed his jacket.

"Seen this yet?" he asked Butterdale.

"No Sir, I was waiting for you to come back from lunch."

"Here you are. Read it out to me, would you?"

Butterdale read the bare facts – state of major organs (nothing there) blood type, approximate time of death, etc. The manner of death was confirmed as strangulation by ligature.

Inspector Erasmus listened intently. When Butterdale had finished reading, he said nothing. He removed his jacket and hung it on the back of his chair. Then he sat down. He swivelled the chair round to look out of the window, over the civic gardens. Butterdale knew he was thinking and did not interrupt him. Instead, he rapidly read through the report again, as if cramming at the last minute for an exam. He rehearsed to himself the key facts about the victim, moving his lips silently as he did so.

Inspector Erasmus slowly rotated his chair another one hundred and eighty degrees, continuing the initial clockwise movement, until once more he was facing his assistant. He put his hands, palm down, on the top of the desk, as if to push himself up, but instead he left them resting there.

"So what do you conclude?"

"Well, we seem to know nothing more than we knew yesterday – nothing more from this report."

"*Au contraire*, we now have our initial suspicion confirmed regarding our victim's manner of death, plus the time of death. But you are right in one respect – it tells us nothing more that is pertinent to the motive for his murder. We need to know about the victim: his work, his background, his friends and family – anything we can find to build a complete picture of him.

What about your initial investigations up at Mournley Woods – anything of interest?"

"Nothing so far, Sir," he replied, but I want to take a closer look at the protestors' camp and the exploration site too."

"Well mind how you go – we don't want to be seen as oppressors of free speech and the right to demonstrate in a democratic society!"

Erasmus was acutely aware of the effect of bad publicity, whether or not there was any veracity in the accusations. Softly, softly, was the policy.

"See if you can find out more about our victim from the site manager – and we need some research on his background. Can we get any help?"

"Not with these latest efficiencies, Sir", Butterdale answered, "but I'll see if I can call in a few favours."

"Okay, see what you can do."

Butterdale left and Erasmus settled down to think. They needed more information and it was no use spending energy in speculation, on unfounded theories, at this early stage in the proceedings. He needed more material to work with. At the same time he worried that, with each passing hour, the trail would be getting colder.

∼

Friday was wet. It had started raining well before breakfast and, according to the forecast, did not look like stopping before supper at the earliest. Erasmus was glad of his old gabardine mac, and his broad-brimmed Australian hat, which he wore like some bushwhacker's talisman. When he arrived at his office, just after half-past eight, Butterdale was already there, though he hadn't yet taken off his cycle clips. His Hi-Vis jacket was on the floor and his cycling helmet was perched on top of one of the filing cabinets. The cuffs on his jacket, and the tips of his shoes, were wet where his waterproofs had failed to protect him fully.

"Sir, we've got some extra support. The request to Department 'C' has turned up trumps – well, they've given us an extra pair of hands, at any rate, for the next two weeks."

"Better than nothing, I suppose," Erasmus replied. "When do we get him?"

"*Her*, Sir. She's waiting next door in the interview room."

"Oh, right. Better show her in then."

WPC Wright was neither tall nor short, had hazel-coloured hair, and spoke with an accent that might have been somewhere in the Borders but could equally well have been further north. Inspector Erasmus greeted her in a friendly manner, as he might any other new colleague, regardless of rank. She immediately warmed to him. She already knew him by reputation but he seemed smaller than she had expected – like the person on television who you see on the street and discover is really not as tall as they appear. She felt at once that she was going to enjoy this posting.

Inspector Erasmus was unorthodox but methodical, in his own way, and was happy to use the tools to suit his purpose. On this occasion he suggested they draw up a mind-map – not so much to describe what they knew so far, as to highlight where the gaps in their knowledge still lay. By the time they had completed this process – not more than fifteen minutes at the most – they were ready to assign tasks to themselves and to begin their research. At this stage they decided to see what they could find out on the Net and carry out a time limited fact search. They would look at the exploration business and the company's backers, finances, etc. They would find out what the environmental line was in the radical press and the key issues. And they would reconvene to pool their findings. They would then decide where to concentrate their efforts, in terms of more detailed investigation, and in what order of priority they would undertake to do this. WPC Wright was pleased to be given an opportunity to show what she could contribute. She would make a start on the business background.

Butterdale would talk to a few contacts – some back up in town – and glean what he could by that means. Erasmus, not excluding himself from the project, was keen to find out more about the murdered man's personal life and how his work affected that in any way. Was he usually away from home for work or was that only occasionally? Did he always work in the UK or did he travel, and if so where and when?

In this way the investigation began to bootstrap itself and get off the ground. It would build a comprehensive picture; it would examine the tiniest anomaly and capture any and every clue.

~

By the time they reconvened they had discovered quite a lot about their subject, and Glaston Exploration, the specialist company he had worked for. The personal details too were starting to shape into something three dimensional.

Name: Robert Marston
Occupation: Mining Engineer
Age: 39
Marital Status: Single

Over the last five years had worked abroad, for all but the last three months, in: Afghanistan, Botswana, Chile, Iraq, Egypt, Kenya, and Mongolia. Most recently Marston had been working in Egypt.

He had a rented flat in Hackney and owned a modest vehicle – a Saab 9-3. He also had a pilot's licence.

He had no previous, but the Met reported, unofficially, that he had been on their peripheral radar on one occasion – something to do with smuggling, but the information was sketchy.

He had qualified in 1998 from the Royal School of Mining and had a Masters in Applied Geology from the Cranfield Institute of Technology.

They had a picture of the man, as he was when still alive. But they needed to know more. They needed information about the circles he moved in, the people he knew, and the people who knew him. They continued their allotted investigations.

8. Siobhan

Siobhan Wright rehearsed the meeting with her father: it would be awkward; it would be undemonstrative; it would be full of the memory of unintended wounds. It would be difficult. She was not looking forward to it but knew she must make the effort – if only for her own sake – to purge the ghosts of the past and prevent them from becoming ever present demons.

It was difficult. She caught the airport bus into town and went straight to her hotel. She had never imagined she would be lodging in the New Town, not far from the Scottish National Portrait Gallery in Queen Street. She knew the area well; she had often been to concerts and shows at the Assembly Rooms, especially during the Fringe Festival. But that was some while ago now and, anyway, she had work to do.

She was here to visit an elderly lady who lived in Musselburgh, to the east of Edinburgh. She had already written to her to ask if she might visit and had then spoken briefly on the phone. Miss McPhairson seemed a cheerful person and said she would be happy to receive a visitor. Siobhan felt guilty that she had assumed the pretence of being a journalist writing an article on Scottish social history. She had said she wanted to interview Miss McPhairson about her family memories and living through the war. This was in part true – but it was not entirely so. Tomorrow she would take a taxi to Musselburgh but, this evening, she would walk down Leith Road to the harbour, a long straight walk, downhill, of about a mile; she would find somewhere to eat and catch a cab back into town.

There might even be a tram now. Much had changed about Edinburgh; much had changed in her life. Fate had taken the girl out of Edinburgh . . .

She changed her mind. She had to get it out of the way. She had to know if she was ever going to be rid of her past.

~

As she approached the cottage she smelled the sweet wild garlic in the woods and she started to cry. It was involuntary, as a flood of childhood memories overcame her all at once, and she was both happy and sad at one and the same time. She stopped and dried her eyes, feeling foolish. She looked around but there was no-one else there.

He did not know she was here. She had not told him. Major Stephen Wright, REME (Retd.) was at home. He sat in the front room of his cottage beyond the River Cramond, overlooking the Firth of Forth. He was scribbling half-heartedly at the cryptic crossword in the Scotsman, lamenting the umwhile demise of his favourite composer 'Conisburgh'. There was a knock at the door. He went to answer it, suspicious of visitors. It was his daughter.

"I suppose you'd better come in then, lass."

"Hello dad."

Siobhan stood for a moment then entered. At a glance nothing seemed to have changed. But she had changed and she tried hard to hold onto this as she felt the over-powering waves of the past swamp over her, knocking the air from her lungs and almost winding her. She sat down by the coal fire.

A photograph of her mother was placed next to the clock on the mantelpiece. It was a black and white picture. The room was neat and clean. Stephen Wright dusted and hoovered every day, with military regularity and precision: everything by numbers. And that was the problem. Life didn't work by numbers – not where people were concerned.

They both began to speak at once – their words the same – both blurting out:

"I'm sorry!"

She rushed over and hugged her dad. He stood stock-still, arms straight at his sides, and then she felt his chest heave and she heard a deep

25

sigh, and she felt him trembling. He put his arms around her and she realised he was crying. She was crying. There was so much pain and relief.

"Your mother was ….."

"I know dad, I loved her too."

"I never understood that, what with all the arguing you two did! Perhaps I was too protective of her, too jealous of anyone else getting her attention."

"No dad, that was my fault. I was headstrong; I was growing up. It wasn't your fault, you know – mum getting ill, I mean. It wasn't anybody's fault."

"It was God's fault – and I curse Him for it!"

"No dad! It's just what happens. Listen. I want to tell you about London."

"Come on, let's make a pot of tea, then you can tell me all you've been up to."

～

She could not stay over even though he offered to make up the spare bed. She had work in the morning and needed to be well prepared for her 'interview'. He drove her to the bus stop, half a mile down the road, and saw her onto the bus back onto town. She turned to wave and he stood and waved back at her.

9. Correspondence

Villa del Ulvio,
Lucca,
Italy.

Dear J.

I'm wondering if you are interested enough – not in your characters, that is certain – but in the plot. It's not exactly flying, and where are the cliff-hangers? I need a reason to carry on reading; you haven't exactly got a page-turner here, have you? I know you don't want to write just another potboiler but you do need to liven it up a bit; it's about time something really happened!

But I must tell you what cousin Rollo is up to. He is engaged in yet another hair-brained scheme! I know I'll never dissuade him – of course that's why I love him so – he's so optimistic and good-hearted. Anyway, he's off to Africa later in the month to work on a new deal with Maartens. Whether it's a question of fools searching for gold I really don't know, but I'm hoping to persuade him to invite me along. Although I have travelled the world, as you know, as far as Australia, I have not had the excuse to visit Africa and its amazing wildlife. Perhaps this will be my chance?

That's all for now - must dash. Looking forward to the next instalment.

Yours Ever,

H.

P.S. Speak soon.

Mournley Cross

Dear H.

I sometimes wonder too. But I think I'm starting to get involved. I feel there is something happening I don't yet know about, something I have not yet realised.

I know you will think I'm exaggerating but this is how it seems to be. Yes, I have a plan – a broad outline at least. Gradually this starts to come into focus. But soon enough the thing takes on a life of its own and the story has 'come to life'. I can think of no other suitable way of putting it.

Be that as it may, I am delighted you will be going to Africa – I mean delighted for you, and thoroughly envious! But we are both busy here – I with my book and Julian with his criminal cases. We were planning to go away late summer – perhaps a few days up in the Lake District. I love the Langdale valley and the Pikes, especially when the days are growing shorter and the skies at night are dark and clear.

Do you remember that year we went camping together? I know we climbed Skiddaw – the 'easy' route! I'd love to go back there and repeat that performance, knees permitting!

If we do get to the Lakes again I will take my Wordsworth, for perhaps one last time. I know you are more of an Augustan – and as I grow older I understand Pope and Byron better now than ever I did before – but my heart belongs to the Romantic vision of Wordsworth and Coleridge; of De Quincey and Charles Lloyd; of the Malay, and the Crocodile Coachman and his beautiful daughter!

Luv

J.

xxx

10. Sam's Courage

Sam liked visiting the camp and only wished he could stay there – but he had work, and his mum to look after. He really enjoyed meeting all the different people, of different ages and from different backgrounds. There were travellers and pensioners, a retired vicar, a gay Buddhist monk, two sisters from the Outer Hebrides who referred to each other as "Sis-One" and "Sis-Two", and there was Treena, who was their spokesperson and natural leader.

Sam was surprised when Treena approached him and drew him away from the camp, suggesting they walk up the hill to survey the site below and perhaps look for orchids on the chalk downs. He was flattered to be noticed and hoped he wasn't obviously blushing. He felt he was talking too much, over-excitedly, but as soon as he realised this Treena said how impressed she was with his knowledge of flora and fauna and she had never realised before how clever he was.

Sam wondered if now was the right time to tell her what he had done to sabotage the drilling. He was full of pride in his achievement. Before he could stop himself he blurted it out. Treena looked at him, said nothing, and then smiled:

"I knew you had it in you," she said, "no one else would act so directly – there is too much talking and not enough doing!"

Then she sat down and signalled for him to join her. Like an eager puppy he happily obeyed. She took his hands and looked into his eyes:

"I want you to do something for me", she said, "I want you to promise you'll tell no one."

Sam was spellbound, like a rabbit hypnotised by a stoat, and sat, mouth open, hardly breathing.

~

Later that day Sam found himself in Worplestone, in a street of red-bricked terraced buildings located behind the railway station. He had committed the address to memory. He was to knock on the door using a coded knock. He would be admitted. He was to ask no questions. There he would collect a packet which he must bring back without telling anyone and without drawing attention to himself. He felt like a secret agent, a spy on an important mission that would determine the outcome of the war – he felt alive!

The man at the door let him in, unsmiling, not saying a word. He led the way into what seemed to be a rather old-fashioned sitting room: flying ducks on the wall, fading floral wallpaper, a Bakelite mantelpiece clock, a fine-mesh brass fireguard in front of an open grate. It was like aunt Aggie's house, the few times he had been to visit. She was dead now. Passed away peacefully in her sleep. Lay undiscovered for a month.

The man left the room. He reminded Sam of one of the bouncers down at the Blue Raven nightclub in town. All he needed was the dark glasses and shiny black boots. Sam looked around and noticed a picture in a frame, an old black and white photograph. It was a picture of children playing in a garden. Siblings or cousins maybe. They had blond hair. He wondered who they were. When had they lived in this house? It must have been sometime before the war at least.

The man returned. He gave Sam a large, bulky envelope. There was no address written on it, only a date stamp in smudged black ink. Then he led Sam out through the kitchen to the back door, pointing to the back gate leading into an alleyway.

Sam was in the garden. He remembered the photograph. The tree was taller, and there was no swing, but it was the same one. The flower borders were unkempt and an old garden shed stood in the corner with its door hanging off the hinges. He glanced back but the kitchen door was shut and the man had gone. Sam stepped out into the alley and made his way home, making sure he was seen by no one till he reached the bridge leading to the Park. Then he marched boldly as if immune from detection, hiding in plain sight.

When he arrived home he checked the soles of his shoes. He scraped the muck off from the left one, then took both off and left them outside the back door. He let himself in and crept quietly upstairs. He heard his mum snoring in the room next door. He needed to hide the package. There was a loose ventilation grille outside his bedroom window which gave access to the small space between the soffit and the eaves. He stuffed the package into this convenient cubby-hole.

The next day he was up early. He skipped breakfast and made his way to the camp, before heading in to work. When he arrived Treena was already at work. She sat by the fire cajoling the embers to come to life again and was waiting to put the billy on to make coffee. Sam sat down on a log opposite and put his coat down on the ground. She smiled; he nodded. She returned to poking the fire. After a few minutes Sam tore himself away from the mesmeric influence of the rising flames, picked up his coat, and stood up to go, leaving behind the packet tucked under the log. Treena stood up too and waved goodbye. Then she moved round the fire and picked up the packet, tucking it into her inside jacket pocket.

11. An Inspector Calls

It was some while since Erasmus had been up to London. He caught a mid-morning train that arrived at Waterloo Station just after noon. He exited by the main staircase and crossed over York Road, then past the arches towards the river. When he got to the river he walked eastwards along the south bank, along the Millennium Way. He noticed that there were beggars once more of the old-school type: bearded and bedraggled alcoholics in the main. There was a time, perhaps some twenty or more years earlier, when young people sleeping rough were prolific – in the Thatcher and Major years. This was followed by a noticeable decline in begging for a while; that was followed by an influx of Eastern Europeans. All this he gathered in a moment of observation, as natural to him as breathing. He observed, he assessed, and he noted – but he tried not to judge, though that was sometimes difficult.

He was making his way to Somerset House, where he had arranged to meet his former Sergeant, Peter Wetherton, in the Café at the Courtauld Institute. There was an exhibition of international photography in the main square – displacing the winter festivities centred on the ice rink. Erasmus headed for the café, seating himself with his back to the wall, by a high window. From this vantage point he watched those who came in and those who left. He put his fingertips together, keeping his eyes open, and dwelt in the moment, meditating without thought. He swept his mind clean of rambling words, of truculent thoughts, and focussed on the salt cellar on the table in front of him. Each crystal was etched with blue and white, and settled at a different angle; each touch upon the tongue brought flavour and life to the palate.

Wetherton sat down opposite, producing two cups of coffee and a slice of flapjack for each of them. He said nothing. Erasmus arose slowly from his self-induced trance and leant forward to smell the subtle aroma of the roasted arabica bean. Wetherton took a bite of his flapjack, and a sip of his coffee, and waited for Inspector Erasmus to surface.

"Good to see you Peter!" declared Erasmus "Sorry about the "hush, hush" and all that."

"Not a problem, Sir – happy to oblige."

"Julian, please."

"If you insist – I'll have to practice!"

Peter Wetherton was perhaps ten or so years younger than Erasmus. The two of them had worked together for over ten years. There was an almost psychic understanding between them, born out of their time spent working together and a natural affinity. Erasmus was a one-off – Wetherton knew this well. He created licence for himself and others. He was trusted by his superiors and he inspired loyalty in his subordinates. Now Wetherton was neither, he did not feel completely comfortable in this new position, at the level of equals.

They got down to business. Erasmus explained his ostensible mission: to deliver the news to the murdered man's family. He needed further background information and hoped to obtain some important indications and clues from his visit. However, he also realised as much would be hidden as made clear, in all likelihood – deliberately or otherwise. A family is rarely a good witness in all respects; some of the deepest secrets lie between the closest members of a family. He needed Peter's help to access Central Data, to see what was already known about the murder victim. He had had a tingling of his sixth sense – a sort of detective's alarm bell – and it told him that there was more to this case than met the eye. If there was any information that might be of use to him in this investigation then he would seek to find it, whatever obstacles presented themselves.

Wetherton had finished his coffee. They stood up and shook hands. Erasmus left his cup half finished. They left together, cutting out onto the Strand. Wetherton walked briskly down towards the Embankment. Erasmus waited and then hailed a cab.

When Erasmus arrived at 36, Barnett Crescent, Lambeth, he paid the cabbie and made sure he got a receipt. The houses were terraced, in red

33

and grey brick, and formed part of a large post-war exercise in providing much needed housing. The London plane trees were mature and the avenues wide. The big red buses plied their trade like unwieldy *vaporetti* released from the prison of their lagoon. He walked along the crescent, looking to see which side the even numbers were located. He crossed over, opposite number 12, and estimated which would be number 36. He saw a single dustbin still on the pavement and located the house he wanted at roughly that distance.

A bell rang in response when he pushed the buzzer. There was no intercom and only a single button to press. He stepped back as he heard someone approaching the door. A woman of about sixty opened the door.

"Yes?" she said.

"Mrs Marston? I'm Inspector Erasmus." He showed her his ID badge.

"Bad news, is it?"

"I'm afraid so."

" 'spected as much. Haven't heard a word in a week or more. 'S'pose you'd better come in then."

Erasmus followed her into the hallway and then they turned right into the front drawing room.

"Cup of tea?"

"Please", he replied.

"Do sit down. Won't be a minute."

Mrs Marston left to make a pot of tea. Erasmus looked around the room. There was a faded photograph on the mantelpiece – a soldier on a troop carrier. The fireplace was period – Edwardian or Victorian, with arts and crafts tiles. There was a single-bar electric fire on the hearth. A Welsh dresser displayed Chinese willow pattern plates and a tarnished silver dish sat on a faded doily. Mrs Marston returned with tea and biscuits.

"Sugar? How did it happen?" she asked.

"No, thanks. I'm afraid he was killed."

"You mean murdered."

"Yes, I'm afraid I do."

"Well, it's no surprise. Too many dealings with unsavoury sorts. I know their type. Criminals, gangsters – that sort."

"How was your son involved?"

"I know he travelled a lot – different countries. I can put two and two together."

"Do you mean he may have been involved in smuggling of some kind?"

She went to the sideboard and rummaged around, then drew out a small plain brown box. Lifting the lid carefully, she raised a fine filigree necklace of gold and brilliant cut diamonds.

"Eighteen carat this, and real diamonds too! What was he doing giving me this? Payment, I reckon, so as I wouldn't say anything."

"Who was he dealing with?"

"That I don't know but it's the *Red Lion* down the road you need to visit if you want to know what goes on round here. By the new Tesco Metro."

Erasmus drank his tea and ate his biscuit, dutifully, like a young boy visiting an aged aunt whose house was dark and smelt odd, as if there were a dead cat in the wainscot concealed by the perfume of too much lavender. He noticed that there was no dust on the mantelpiece or photograph, none even on the lampshade that hung in the middle of the ceiling.

When he left he noticed someone peering from the upstairs window – a slight movement of the net curtain. Either Mrs Marston could bound up the stairs three at a time, or there was someone else in the house too.

He caught the bus back along the wide avenue as far as Waterloo. He alighted by Lower Marsh and walked up the curving access road, on the opposite side of the station from the main exit. Dodging the taxis, he entered near the low-number platforms. With time to wait he picked up the evening paper and took the escalator up to Carluccio's. He had half an hour to wait for the fast train.

～

Erasmus had found himself a window-seat on the shady side and opened his evening paper. He skimmed the main pages for news then turned to the puzzles page. Staring at the Sudoku, he fell into a trance-like state.

35

The facts of the case moved in ever shifting patterns as his subconscious brain sifted and filtered and rearranged things in an apparently arbitrary fashion. In this passive state, with attention to the body's needs reduced to the minimum of breathing, he took dominion over his full conscious and unconscious resources to scour the landscape for signs of something out of place – the tiniest of connections that might form a clue. A snowflake began to grow in his mind's eye, gradually taking shape, then altering shape as it grew larger. Numbers began to flow in lines, viewed from different angles and forming a three-dimensional structure over time. Verb endings melted into strange conjugations and thought was inflected and turned in upon itself. Functions of thought were applied, reflexively, to themselves, in a seemingly infinite hall of mirrors. The patterns repeated, and repeated again. And on the edge of vision another pattern started to emerge and repeat and grow until, like continents they collided.

He woke with a start as the train lurched suddenly to an abrupt halt at its final destination and the tannoy shouted at the passengers to disembark:

"This is God speaking - train terminates here."

Luckily it wasn't his – or anybody else's god. It was only the guard.

12. Jennifer

She knew she had relaxed into a false quietude, one which lacked integrity, but it was nigh on impossible to shift away from it. This in itself was wearying and, somewhere in the back of her mind, she was aware of this. But for now she carried on carrying on and felt as if she were commanded to continue, to endeavour, to persevere.

Julian was a good husband: loyal, considerate, helpful – to the point of annoyance sometimes – and always dependable. But if this was love, it was an unadventurous thing, more a stoical necessity than a Dionysian challenge. She was becoming bored, and the world itself was becoming dull. She hoped she was not entering one of her depressive states – the pills should continue to prevent that, but she was not completely confident. She returned to re-reading the previous chapter of her book, to distract herself. Gradually she realised she had lost herself in the story once again. Her concerns were pushed out of her conscious mind, for the time being.

Julian was away in London on business. He was the telegram that mothers received in wartime, the harbinger of dreadful news. She knew, however, that his nature was compassionate and he bore the duty of human communication willingly and with good grace. Sometimes she envied him his placid nature and his self-sufficiency, but mostly she felt deprived of opportunities for sociable exchange and fulfilment. She knew she should try to do more but she felt isolated. She had 'made her bed', as her mother would have said.

She thought of telephoning her sister, but then thought better of it. Supportive though she was it was not a burden she could share with Becky. She was happy and did not yet know what shadows might fall upon a marriage – she hoped she would never know. Of course she could talk to H. but she was out of the country – texting would not do. She must rely on her own strength, her own stamina and careful self-understanding – there was no one else.

There was no one else except the characters in her book. They looked at her, they seemed to be quizzing her, silently. She told them to stop staring at her. She *ordered* them to stop staring. They turned and walked away and she was alone again.

When she woke it was hardly light but a car's headlights were blazing through a gap in the curtains. The milkman was delivering to a few houses nearby and the taxi was depositing the nurse, returning home from her overnight shift. It was six-thirty in the morning.

Jennifer threw on her dressing gown and put her slippers on, then made her way downstairs to the kitchen to put the kettle on. Everything was neat and clean and tidy. Everything was in its place; everything was in order. Ostensibly – everything visible and external – was in order. She made herself a cup of tea and a piece of toast. She swallowed her daily pills with a glass of water, then pushed them down with the dry toast. The tea was just cool enough now to sip at.

Walking along the hallway she stopped to check the barometer. Pressure falling. Rain. No respite.

She went into the office and sat down at the desk, turning on her computer. She would fill her head with others' thoughts and words and deeds. She would live in their world for an hour or two. She would work.

Of course, settling down to work — like writing thankyou letters — is something that is never easy, yet must be done, though perhaps not in this day and age. But I will let her try to work and she may write something – I don't know. But I'm sure she won't remember any of this.

She woke from her work and got up to make coffee. In the kitchen, hanging by the back door, she noticed the key to the shed. She decided she would mend the puncture in the front tyre of her bicycle. Bowl of water, teaspoons, puncture-kit (chalk, glue, patches) – she had all she needed. She had a purpose.

The cat dropped by to see what she was doing. It offered its assistance, rubbing itself against her arms and legs as she knelt to work on the wheels.

When she ran the inner tube through the bowl of water to find the air bubbles that would pin-point the puncture, Cheshire dipped his paw in the water and tried to catch the bubbles. She laughed. The cat looked at her as if she were doing something odd. Then he stood up, raised his tail erect, and walked away haughtily.

The sun had dispelled the early cloud and it promised to be a fine day, despite the barometer's pessimistic forecast. Jennifer was glad to be up and about in the open air. She switched off her mobile phone, carrying it only in case of an emergency. It raised her spirits. Her head felt clearer and her body sprung with rhythm and energy. She headed off towards Mournley Woods, edging the stream towards the village before turning off up a small track that crossed the canal by a small arched stone bridge. This was where the tow-horses would cross from one side to the other. There were no narrow boats today; all was quiet. The sudden flash of a kingfisher's blue dash caught her eye and she laughed with surprise.

After about half an hour she came to Mournley Wood, which lay in a hollow below the ancient yews of Queens Dale and the old hanging tree below Beacon Hill. It was off the beaten track but now a muddy scar had been drawn from the B-road in a large arcing loop, skirting the edge of the chalk pits. She stopped cycling and listened. There were no lorries or plant at work; all was quiet except for the laugh of a green woodpecker and the buzz of a bee in the flowers. She looked more closely and saw that it was actually struggling in a web. The web's designer had woken and was moving in quickly, then it stopped. In that moment she made her decision. She broke the web and freed the bee, depriving the spider of its meal. She felt a mixture of ethical justification and guilt, as if her intervention was, in a perfect sense, unnatural.

She got off her bike and began to push it along the track. Silver birch trees and yellow gorse bushes, scented like coconut, hemmed her in on either side. She heard a Yellowhammer's *"little bit of bread and (no) cheeeese!"* And then the whole earth shook and a deafening roar crashed through the trees. She smelled burning. She smelled something else but could not identify it. He heart was pounding and the she heard the blood pumping in her veins. She ran to the crest of the hill and looked down upon the fracking operation and the nearby protestors' camp, about a quarter of a mile further east. Smoke and flames were billowing from the fracking site. As she drew closer she could see people were rushing about in a state of panic, whilst others stood still as if in shocked disbelief.

She called the emergency services on her mobile phone, despite having no signal, unwittingly testing the availability of 'Emergency Calls Only'.

13. Sam's Moment

He had received a txt from Treena –

"mt me @ Top Pit 9 2nyt".

By half past seven he was already on his mountain bike and heading across to the old chalk pits above the Long Straight. He saw a jay fly low into the oak and a pheasant rushed into the hedge as he approached. His heart was pumping and the air was cold in his lungs; his legs were aching but he ignored the pain and engaged the hill standing on the pedals and weaving side to side. Each pull was an effort that dragged him, slowly, nearer to the top of the hill. Sometimes, when it was late and he was cycling home, he would fall asleep – he knew this only because he remembered setting off home and the next thing he was lying in his bed and the owls were noisy in the lane and the street lamps were dimmed. Then he would fall asleep again. Now, he heaved, the last pumping at the pedals, side to side, and he reached the top of the hill. He stopped pedalling and free-wheeled along the road along to the chalk pits.

This was his chance. Was this the moment? Would Treena really see him as an equal, someone she could … He tried to stop himself thinking about it. He hoped he wouldn't make a fool of himself.

Treena waited. Alone. She had a penknife and whittled idly at a hazel twig. She waited.

Sam dismounted and lay down his bicycle in the hedge, where it would not be easily seen from the road. He approached the last few yards to the chalk pit on foot. He caught sight of her high up on the rim of the pit by a storm felled beech tree. Quickly he scrambled up the dell, grabbing at roots and ivy, till he reached the edge where Treena sat, waiting for him. She smiled.

"Come and sit here on this log, next to me."

Sam obeyed.

"You can see the whole valley from here, right across the woods and as far as Hopeton Hill."

Treena pointed eastwards and Sam followed the contours and the colours of the land as she described them.

"This is what we're fighting for. This is why we must stop the destruction of our land. I need your help again. Will you help me?

Sam stuttered and nodded.

"Good. Then I can trust you. That other recent mission was just a test and now you've proven yourself. I need you to do something else for me. I'll explain as we walk."

They got up off the log and walked along a track leading up and away from the chalk pit, away from Mournley Woods, till they found themselves at the door to an old stone cottage on the edge of Brinkley Ridge. It was an isolated spot but, on entering the hut, Sam noticed the smell of incense. Gradually, as his eyes grew used to the dim light, he saw a fireplace and a small table in the corner of the room. Treena took his hand – "this is where I live when I'm not down at the camp", she said. Then she led him to the room at the back and let him make love to her.

~

It was dark. Well past midnight. Sam stood at the back of the lorry. They were about to open the container. He had a small haversack. He gave it to the man next to him. After a few minutes it was handed back to him. They closed the tailgate, locked it, and ran back to the cab. The truck drew away as the man scrambled up into the passenger's seat. Sam turned and walked quickly back to where he had left his bicycle. He went along the canal path, riding without lights, and made his way home. A cat darted across the path and he nearly ran it over. When he got home he hid the haversack in the soffit, as before, and then got ready for bed. When he lay down on his bed he was buzzing, with images of strange meetings in strange houses, and mysterious deals, running through his head unbidden. Eventually he had to resort to talking his body to sleep from his toes upwards.

The following morning he took the sack with him to work. After work he cycled straight to the camp to see Treena. She was sitting with some others by a fire where a kettle was boiling. They were drinking herbal tea which Sam didn't really like, but he had some anyway. When Sis-One and Sis-Two got up and left them there alone he took the opportunity to pass the bag he was carrying over to Treena. She smiled and thanked him. He had to be back for tea and waited a moment then walked back to his bike and rode away. When he looked back, over his left shoulder, she had gone.

Two days later Sam was having his dinner and watching the news – there had been an explosion at the Mournley Woods fracking site. He felt sick. He retched but there was nothing but liquid – a cup of sweet tea an hour earlier. He knew, he knew now what had been in the bag he had given to Treena. He believed in the cause – but this? He knew it was not what he meant. Treena? Was it an accident? Surely something went wrong – it should have happened when no one was on site. He had to know.

∽

There had been an explosion at the drilling site. Two workers had been killed and several others injured. It was not yet clear what had happened but Erasmus feared the worst. His fears were confirmed by the Chief Fire Officer:

" You can see certain fragments here, and here – we've determined the centre of the explosion. The bomb was planted by the main rig and a timer was used to detonate it. More than that – you'll have to wait for forensics."

Erasmus thanked him. This was not good, not good at all.

∽

The camp would be under close surveillance now – under lock-down most probably. Sam decided to go up to the cottage, thinking Treena might be there. The cottage was dark. The door was locked. She was not there.

He retraced the path they had taken a few days before, back towards the chalk pits. As he approached he could see Treena sitting on the log overlooking the pit. She was rolling a spliff.

"Want some?" she asked, offering him the spliff as he stepped out of the trees and came towards her.

"No! What happened? What did you do?"

She lit up and took a cool breath of the sweet weed.

"Don't be like that. We have to stop this shit – you know that."

"Not like this – people are dead!"

"It's war, silly. We're at war. Look come here."

She held out her hand towards him. He did not move. She got up and stepped towards him, still holding out her hand. He stepped backwards. Again she stepped forwards.

He felt himself slip but it was as if he were watching someone else – he felt a sensation like butterflies. He saw a hand reaching towards him, then pushing him. He saw her smile and he screamed silently.

14. More Correspondence

Dear J,

I am fascinated by the patchwork quilt approach afforded by the medium of word processing — more precisely the ability to cut & paste, to re-order sections, or return to previous unfinished chapters for completion, and the overall freedom this allows you to construct your story in a non-sequential manner. Of course the result is then read in a particular order, as defined by the chapter and page numbers. Sometimes I do feel that this sequence could equally well be read in a variable order. Certainly I have read it in its evolving state and seen some of these slips and shifts.

(There — you see? I have started this section before you have even started the previous chapter. Do forgive me).

As I've started, you will — I hope — let me continue? I think you've got something here. No doubt it will need polishing but don't give up. I suspect you may have something here which is not your usual fare but may prove to be more successful.

Looking forward to your visit.

Yours Ever,

H.

Mournley Cross

Dear H,

Thanks for your insight. I will of course take on board what you say and ignore your every suggestion!

I am beginning to get a clearer picture of where things might go and how they should proceed. I have known, almost since the beginning, what I wish to include in terms of the overall direction and content of the plot, but only now have I begun to see how it might all come together. Of course I must give nothing away — only to say that it is much clearer to me now where the story is heading. The individual strands will be woven together (in all probability) and a conclusion will be reached. And yet I am still by no means certain that I will reach such a conclusion. I somehow suspect there is something that will disrupt or derail me. Let's see what happens.

In the meantime I shall continue to explore both character and plot, to see where they lead. Rest assured I have no overall master plan — certainly none in any detail, only the hint of an overall approach to things and an inclination to bend this 'reality' to suit my purposes.

I feel as if there are many stories — a number of lives — taking place simultaneously - and I am merely selecting them at random, or trying to impose a meaning, some semblance of order, upon them. And it's great fun skipping among the chapters and adding something here, and changing something there. It is as if it's all happening at once!

Looking forward to seeing you in Lucca!

Luv,

J.

xxx

46

Dear J.

Spring has reached London — your beloved Wordsworth himself would admire our St James' Park daffodils! I still have my winter coat on the hallway peg but yesterday it was so warm I had to go and unearth a jacket from the wardrobe.

You must listen to T.P. on Radio 4's "The Modern Muse". He talks about the visual imagination and the creation of a sense of place.

If you were to ask me who were my favourite writers, I would have to include: Fanny Burney, George Eliot, and Virginia Woolf. On reading them, immediately I am transported in time and place to a moment, to a garden or a beach, to another world — and I know it; it is as present to me as if I were there.

And it is not affected; it is natural, this seemingly effortless working of imagination, this including the reader as confidant. Of course all three writers work essentially in this same vein but the depth and colour, and the self-awareness and distancing, varies. For one it is deliberately removed; for another it is core to the 'truth' of the narrative with the narrator as first-hand witness, participant and re-creator of events; and for yet another, it is the ability to create and inhabit a myriad of characters, human or animal — a 'negative capability' worn lightly.

At this point I should give examples but to do so would mean returning to the texts and I'm afraid I'm too busy for that just now. Anyway, I thought you might like to know that the experience of "being present" is something I find most fascinating.

Well, that's all for now. Will phone next week with details of the concert — do hope you can come.

Yours ever,

H.

15. A Matter of Jurisdiction

On Wednesday morning the Assistant Chief Constable summoned Erasmus to his office.

"Ah Julian, do come in!"

Immediately Erasmus knew something was up – too familiar by far, not his usual formal self. What was he up to?

"Look, I'll get straight to the point. No aspersions. No criticism, implicit or explicit. Nothing like that. Orders from above, you see?"

Erasmus didn't see but waited to be enlightened.

"For once not even a resourcing issue!"

He laughed at his own joke. Erasmus smiled tactfully.

"Not sure myself, really. Thing is it's out of our hands, see? Bally spooks are on to it. Don't know why – didn't ask. Too important for the likes of us, you know."

"What, Scotland Yard you mean? "

"Couldn't say, but – between you and me – wouldn't be surprised if it was higher up the pecking order. Official Secrets Act an' all that, you know!"

Erasmus didn't know but realised he would learn no more in detail. He had one question.

"So what does this mean for my investigation?"

"Handover all you've got so far – the murder and the bombing – and do no more. Someone will be coming in this afternoon to debrief you. Give 'em what they want, old chap, won't you?"

"Yes Sir, of course."

Back in his office, Erasmus pondered. Clearly more to this than meets the eye, he thought. Still, if that's how they want to play it.

Butterdale was miffed and PC Wright was obviously none too happy, to say the least.

"We'll just have to make the best of it. It's disappointing, I know, but those are the orders. Right, so where does that leave us?"

No one spoke.

"Right, fresh air!" he exclaimed, "That's what we need – come on, get your coats – team exercise!"

And so saying he led them out of the office and down to the Chichester Canal, where they struck out along the tow-path heading west towards Birdham. There were a few early holiday-makers negotiating the locks in their narrow boat but the waterway was generally very quiet. Erasmus admired the solid engineering of the locks and the simplicity of the mechanism.

As they walked along they found the slower pace of life on the water relaxed them mentally and physically. They walked along in silence. When they came to the next lock they crossed over, regaining the tow-path on the other side. At Birdham they stopped by the quayside at the marina. Looking across the estuary they could see a large white marquee. A wedding was being celebrated and everyone was dancing to the sound of a ceilidh band under the encouraging and instructive commands of an amplified caller. Erasmus danced a mental jig for a moment and then said:

"Right. Let's get back to work."

They turned around and retraced their steps back into town. The wedding feast continued and eventually the strains of the fiddle and the accordion died away until only the bass and drums were audible, and then there was musical silence and the familiar noise of traffic.

～

On Thursday of that same week they were each interviewed by a man called Evans. Evans was a frosty man. No glimmer of 'soft' skills, rather a stickler for detail and procedure. He spoke to Erasmus first, and then briefly to the others. He informed them that he reserved the right to ask them further questions at a later date should the need arise but, in the meantime, the case would be entirely conducted by his office (whatever that was) and he reminded everyone that it was now a security matter and not to be discussed further.

Of course the outcome was otherwise, as is only to be expected where people are told what they may and may not do. Later that afternoon, Inspector Erasmus treated his junior officers to a round of ice creams and a surprise announcement. There was something else for them to follow up on: the death of a young man near Mournley Chalk Pits, whilst not immediately suspicious, nevertheless it needed investigating. The Assistant Chief had kindly found the team another distraction to take their minds off the bombing and the murder, which had been stolen by higher powers.

"I'd like us to treat this as any other case: full background on the deceased: contacts, sympathies, schooling. Assume nothing. We will concentrate fully on *this case*," stated Inspector Erasmus.

"Why haven't they taken this case away? It's not far from the exploration site and the protestors' camp. I would have expected them to include it."

"Indeed, but they haven't. I have my suspicions but, if we are to do this properly then we need to worry solely about our case."

"Has his mother been interviewed yet?" asked WPC Wright.

"No, not yet. I'm just off now."

"May I come with you, Sir? It may help."

"Please do."

Inspector Erasmus and WPC Wright set off, leaving Butterdale to look into the lad's background.

Erasmus was already too familiar with this type of duty and did not relish the challenge; having Wright with him might provide him with the opportunity to observe, more so than if he were the sole messenger. As they drove to the house he thought back on his visit to London and his interview with RM's mother. She had been strangely disengaged – perhaps it had been the shock. But there was definitely another person in the house. He made a mental note to go back, under some pretext – something he had forgotten to ask. He wanted a second look. Something niggled him and he could not put his finger on what it was.

Sam's mother, Mrs Grainger, Mrs Susan Grainger, had hardly had time to digest the news. She was in a state of shock and the doctor had offered her a sedative – which she had refused. Her neighbour was with her, a Mrs Albright, an older lady, practical and sensible, it seemed. She went to make a pot of tea.

Erasmus began the questioning but then let Wright take over whilst he listened and observed. He sipped unconvincingly at the sweet tea. Mrs Albright stood by the door to the kitchen, discretely, at a distance, ready to move to Mrs Grainger's aid should she be needed. It was clear that Susan Grainger was a self-sufficient person. She did not like to be out of control or appear to be at all weak in any way. After all, she had had to be self-sufficient these many years – her feckless husband had left her with a baby who was only just starting to cut his teeth. But the loss of her son, her only child, had knocked a lot of the stuffing out of her. Her eyes were smudged and her complexion was mottled red and white, a blotchiness that betrayed her distress. Nevertheless, she kept a stiff upper lip during the interview and answered clearly all the questions put to her.

It was evident, Erasmus thought, that she – like so many mothers – knew little enough about what their children got up to. It was not surprising, but in this case it had had tragic consequences. She was, of course, inclined to blame herself – from some invented oversight or some lack of care – but that was not the case and she would come to realise it, in time. At the moment she was in obvious pain. Erasmus was glad that his WPC had conducted the interview. He had learnt much.

He had discovered that the boy had, lately, departed from his usual routine – had been keeping odd hours. Presumably he had been seeing a girl – best ask his friends about that. He discovered that the boy had a computer and they might find something useful there. He discovered he needed to know more.

Butterdale and WPC Wright together would interview the protestors – nothing about the explosion, but solely about the boy. Did anyone there know him? Did anyone recognise him? He would get the Forensic Data Analysis team to examine the lad's laptop.

Erasmus was troubled. Two things in particular concerned him: one thing political (small 'p' etc.) and the other pertaining to the death of this young man. The options for the latter included: suicide (right age);

51

accident (probable); murder (possible). As to the political matter, he was accustomed to giving ground where necessary and only choosing to fight the battles he thought he could win – unless on a fundamental point of moral principle – and even then he had learnt to be careful.

∿

Butterdale was puzzled by the approach Inspector Erasmus was taking to the case. He thought it over-cautious.

"Well, I wouldn't claim my approach is cautious, exactly," he explained to Butterdale, "But it is selective. I am aware that I am able to choose how to react – rather than just react – in any given situation. Of course the intellectual awareness of this is not the same as putting it into practice, as you will learn. But it is a good start, at least.

∿

Erasmus was suddenly aware of a hiatus in events but did not know what it was or what had caused it. It was something he sensed, rather than being able to provide evidence for. But he was not wrong thereby, as time would prove. He felt that there were things currently outside his field of vision: some were as stated by the Assistant Chief Constable, whilst others were of a completely different nature and, as yet, still to be discerned in any distinct shape or form.

16. Harriet

Harriet Gordon had known Jennifer since their school days. They had grown up together. They had gone up to Oxford together, though they were at different colleges. In their first year they had been too busy to spend much time with each other. In the second year they found themselves in the same lectures on the Scottish Enlightenment. In their third and final year they had shared a small terraced house together in Jericho, not far from the centre of town.

After graduation they both moved to London and shared a flat in Camden. Jennifer had become engaged to Julian. Harriet had a number of boyfriends, but none lasted. She spent a lot of her time socialising with her cousin Rollo, who was a few years older than her. Rollo was adventurous, outgoing, gregarious and gay. He was great company, if occasionally a bit outrageous – that's probably why Harriet liked him so much.

Harriet had detected a shift in Jennifer's mood lately – not just in the tone of her writing in her new book, but in their correspondence also. Occasionally they would talk on the phone or send emails – neither liked so-called "social media" and eschewed it. Most often they preferred writing old-fashioned letters, as if they might preserve this ancient art form by their own modest endeavours.

She was looking forward to going to Africa with cousin Rollo and thought of inviting Jenny – after all he would be busy much of the time and she would like a companion. After all she had been planning to come to stay with her in Lucca later in the year.

She sent her an invitation. No rush. She would hear from her soon. Then she set about organising the clothes she had already, and deciding what new ones she would need for the trip. Harriet had already checked her vaccinations and already had her Hepatitis A jab. She would need to start the prophylactic malaria course soon.

Though by no means a writer herself, Harriet was, nevertheless, a voracious reader of all the books that appeared on the various book-prize shortlists, not only the winners. In a sense she was indiscriminate about her reading but found it immensely enjoyable in spite of that fact, or perhaps because of it. She had never settled into a particular genre or a specific author. She had never re-embraced the same style for its own sake; she had always sought to be surprised by something new and different. In another sense, by virtue of her disparate reading, she had developed a refined sense of the well-written and what made it so. This was certainly something Jenny admired in her and one of reasons she was happy to use her as her willing and trusted touchstone.

Picking up the evening paper from the corner shop, Harriet decided to take a walk in the park to watch the nannies and their charges feeding the ducks. It was a warm day but there was still a breeze. She wore her long green and blue check coat, with a silk scarf over her hair and tied under her chin, in a nineteen-forties style. She had always liked this fashion – her grandmother was a stylish woman who encouraged her liking for clothes and dressing up. Even now she enjoyed the war-time recreations that took place every year at Pickering and would drag cousin Rollo along in his RAF pilot's uniform. Despite his annual protestations Rollo clearly enjoyed himself as together they made a very handsome couple and always drew attention.

About half way round the lake she stopped and sat down on an unoccupied bench. She opened the paper, giving it a shake. There had been an explosion at the fracking site next to the village where her best friend lived, by the coast in Sussex. A moment later she received a text from Jenny, asking to talk that evening. She had important news about events and they must talk.

Harriet was curious but not entirely surprised. She knew that her friend was not prone to over-dramatisation – at least, not in real life – but nevertheless she felt wary on this occasion. There was something in the tone of the brief message that made her feel slightly ill at ease. She was not sure why.

19. Sir Lionel Wilberforce

On this fine May morning, Sir Lionel Wilberforce was standing by the window in his modern office, overlooking the Thames. Sir Lionel was the Head of MI5. He had been the head of MI5 for almost ten years. He enjoyed the role and the responsibility; he enjoyed his position. It provided him with a sense of purpose, as if he were doing something important and meaningful. In his professional life this was certainly the case; in his personal life he sometimes doubted it.

Sir Lionel did not direct field agents himself but rather through his subordinates. He hadn't run field agents himself since he took the top job. This distance had the peculiar effect of stabilising his emotions and helped him invoke a stiff upper lip. However, he had, perhaps foolishly, made an exception in this particular case: Marston was one of his. He was in fact the only operative out in the field he controlled – or rather had been. Soon he would be lodged in another field, more permanently, pushing up the daisies. Sir Lionel was shocked at his own inappropriate sense of humour! He felt he needed to get a grip, both on himself and the situation. What had begun as an attempt to revive his rusty skills was, quite unexpectedly, soon to become a question of national importance. Of course he did not know that yet, but he did not want his dabbling in operations to be widely known and criticised. He knew his enemies would use it against him. He needed to find a way to play it down or, if not actually cover it up, then to take complete control of it. He turned from the window and marched back to his desk.

"In for a penny, in for a pound!" he said to himself.

$\sim$

Lionel had never forgiven himself. It was he who had suggested Jennifer as a *Possible*, or rather a *Highly Probable*. He was in charge of recruitment at the time and she was an obvious candidate. But somehow it had all gone wrong. The tried and tested process of seduction that he always employed had not succeeded. His will had not prevailed. His 'advances' had been rejected. He had set his store on this special recruit and felt the loss, to the Service, deeply. He still held a soft spot for her. More than that. He was still in love with her, though he may not have known it. All he knew was that it was all damnably difficult. He wished he could turn back the clock, make amends in some way. But he knew it was too late now. If only Jennifer hadn't started to write this blessed book of hers. It threatened to reveal too much and that really would not do. He could not allow it.

20. OHMS

The weather had taken a turn for the worse. Yesterday's sunny spring day had given way to meteorological phenomena more suited to, well any time of year in the UK really. The skies were grey and it was drizzling persistently. Sir Lionel was not amused by the latest turn of events, quite apart from the weather. He had needed to reclaim his deceased field officer from the local police, and had succeeded in doing so only after pulling several very important strings. Matters seemed to be getting out of hand – exponentially, in every direction – like the explosion of some spontaneous singularity. He had no inclination to disappear into a wormhole and reappear on the other side of the world – Belize perhaps, or Mumbai – if he were lucky. St Helena was probably the best he could hope for.

Dispelling this negative train of thought with an effort of will (Wil' by name and Will by nature) he consciously exerted the *Übermensch* and took a new grip on the situation.

"Ms Jenkins. Get hold of Raffington for me, would you, please?"

A well-trained voice answered over the intercom in the affirmative. A few minutes later Raffington appeared.

"Ah Charles, just the man! Do sit down. Drink? No? Well you won't mind if I do?"

He poured himself a small whisky on the rocks, a fine Western Isles malt.

"I'm afraid we find ourselves on a bit of a sticky wicket."

"How's that?" replied Raffington.

Sir Lionel ignored the intended pun and pressed on.

"We had the police calling to see 'Mrs Marston' – had to set the thing up pretty damn quick, I can tell you. Still, I think he bought it."

Raffington raised an eyebrow:

"So what's the problem – why do you need me?"

Sir Lionel tugged at the double cuffs on each sleeve in turn, first the left and then the right – a mannerism indicative of his having reached a decision. He moved to the window overlooking the Thames, his back towards Raffington. Then he turned around and walked slowly back to his desk, placing both hands palm down.

"This is what we're going to do – our friends will be none the wiser."

When Sir Lionel had completed his briefing – almost – he remembered one last thing:

"And don't underestimate her. The chaps at Oxford tried to recruit her but she declined our offer."

Raffington was amused by this challenge. He rather fancied that he was fool enough to fool even the brightest talent. He would enjoy this mission.

～

All this was surveyed, at the same time, by another. There were no listening devices, no micro-bugs, no discrete spies strategically placed, no one guarding the nation's Guards. There was merely a presence, an imagination, a weaver of intertwining narratives who sought to remain unseen but could not resist the temptation, on occasions such as this, to join in the fun. Having signed the Official Secrets Act himself (not once, but twice) he felt entitled to make the most of this opportunity.

～

Meanwhile, Erasmus was still piecing together the elements – the half hints and scrapes of rendering – in an effort to contrive a unity of events, an explanation that would conform to the normal basis of reality as generally agreed by experience and acted upon, to a greater or lesser extent, by one and all. He knew – of course he knew – there was more to things than met the eye. He knew all was not as it seemed. And he knew it was his job, regardless, to bring a focus to bear that would solve the problem – not only the murders, but the problem, as it now stood, and as he suspected he had not yet fully appreciated.

~

The characters stand poised: who will make the next move? What consequences, foreseen and unforeseen, will this have? Not even the Author knows – not yet. Erasmus suspects he has still to know, that there was something still to be known, but he has not yet fathomed what it might be.

21. An Act of Passion

He knew he would need to get closer to Jennifer. He knew the best
way to achieve this was not the direct approach but rather through
a trusted intermediary. Who better than her friend Harriet Gordon?
The question was: how to befriend her? Again, the answer was: through
another intermediary.

The growth in popularity of social media has given rise to the popular
myth that we are never more than a few clicks away from someone we
know. Through a linked chain of friends, and friends of friends, we can
reach our destination – though this type of pyramid scheme would seem
to reach to more people than exist on the planet, nevertheless we follow
its links till, inevitably, we find who we are looking for.

The intermediary he chose – found rather – was a woman at the
British Library who attended the same Pilates class as Harriet. He had
been cultivating this resource casually for several months now – no
particular reason, just keeping in practice. It was the sort of luck that
Raffington seemed able to conjure, almost at will.

But he had not counted on Harriet. She was amazing. He could
not look beyond her. Quite unwittingly Harriet was protecting Jennifer
from the unwanted advances of MI5 in general, and Charles Raffington
in particular.

∼

It was late in the evening and getting dark now. Charles and Harriet
walked along the Embankment together, as they had done the week
before. This time it was just the two of them. Charles played the attentive
fool, making her laugh unwittingly, and knocking her guard down with

effortless ease. She became angry with herself for this weakness. Why had she let herself be drawn into this? Why did she feel tempted?

She could not help herself. It was not *ennui* – quite the opposite. It was as if she felt alive again. She hadn't realised how un-alive she had become to the routine of her daily existence. She felt alone, unhindered, responsible to no one but herself.

The moment came: a moment of weakness, it is commonly said. But she felt it to be a moment of empowerment, of self-will exerted, of release from all unnecessary convention. The day had been warm and bright: the daffodils tossed their heads in St James's Park and songbirds busied themselves with song and with each other. The hotel was refined – a boutique near Victoria. The styling was classical, in white Portland stone. The staff were discrete and self-effacing. There was nothing sullied, no sense of impropriety or guilt. She felt perfectly in control and at ease. She had chosen this moment; she had brought things to this point. Their union was sudden. It was physical and powerful, despite their own individual knowledge of the roles they played.

In the morning they made love again – a solemn love, a slow and burning passion, rekindled from the embers of their earlier desperation. They left together. She took a taxi to the mainline station; he walked to Victoria to catch a bus to Camden.

It was a week later and Jennifer had called Harriet and left a message. She had wanted to talk urgently; she had called her to explain everything. At first Harriet was perplexed, worried that her friend had at last lost the plot as it were. Whether she believed it or not didn't seem to matter - it was her friend's reality that counted and she acknowledged that. She would call her back later. Now she had to get ready; she was due to meet Charles later that afternoon. They would promenade beside the Thames, perhaps taking in the pictures at the Courtauld Institute, now located in Somerset House. She had been looking forward to seeing him again.

Raffington saw her from a distance, before she saw him. He used this to his advantage to see how she was behaving – agitated or calm? Impatient or relaxed? He was looking for any sign that she might be on to him. He knew this was unlikely but, given the nature of the situation, he felt it best to take more than the usual precautions. He could not afford to trust that a renegade Author would not detect his part in affairs.

They exchanged chaste kisses twice, one on each cheek, and smiled nervously. She blushed a little and he averted his gaze so as not to embarrass her. Together they began to walk across Waterloo Bridge and towards Somerset House. It was early evening, after rush hour, and the traffic was quieter now; it was possible to make it across to the other side of the road within only a modicum of diligence. Twice a week the Courtauld Institute opened in the evenings, seeking to extend its cultural offering in competition with the many other distractions of the capital. Inevitably they made their way to the impressionist paintings to admire the Monets and Renoirs; there was something seductive in their play of light and warmth and colour. She remembered an earlier time when the paintings had been housed near Holborn and it had been necessary to take the lift to the upper floors to view these treasures. She had an aunt who had served as PA to the CEO of Courtaulds and wondered what had become of her. Was she still living in Surbiton? Her younger sister might know – she kept up with everyone.

Charles was rather obviously admiring a work by Pissarro, as if he felt obliged to do so. His appreciation seemed to her to lack sincerity, as if he were reciting some textbook quote, googled from the Net in dutiful manner, rather than heartfelt. Perhaps it was just an awkwardness, one that he usually sought to disguise with his clowning? Perhaps it was something less innocent, part of his plan to engage her and to get at Jennifer?

They took coffee in the cafeteria on the lower ground floor. She refused a slice of cake and he selected a piece of flapjack. When they had finished they made their way back across Waterloo Bridge. The sky was orange to the West and the city was beginning to come to life again after its late afternoon lull. They took the steps down onto the South Bank and walked side by side, hands in pockets, towards the Tate Modern.

Harriet knew she was hypervigilant – she could hear her heart pounding in her ears – and she noticed everything, every detail: the child licking at an ice cream and stuffing it into the cornet before it melted, the dog sniffing from tree to tree, the juggler setting up his multi-coloured stall, the red-eyed drunk, with grey and matted hair, coughing in the subway. It was getting dark now. An interstitial space imposed itself between the clarity of daylight and the sharpness of artificial illumination at night. Though still warm for the time of year, she drew up her collar against the cold. But the cold came from within her. Her thermostat was awry; suddenly she felt a flush swarm over her heated body like the tow and drag of a red-flagged tide.

Everything seemed to flow in slow motion. She moved with alarming speed. She watched herself as she lurched forward and pushed Charles over the parapet. He tumbled like a ragdoll into the swift and muddy waters of the Thames, screaming soundlessly, as dark as a butterfly, as heavy as a feather.

She turned and started to walk the short distance back to the Queen Elizabeth Halls. Everyone seemed frozen in motion – even the juggler with all three objects spinning in the air – nothing moved except her. She was as fast and lithe as a mountain lion. She was as gathered as the coil that feeds the spring. She was moving like a flame that leaps freely from one tree to another. She noticed an elation welling up from somewhere deep inside of her. Gradually she began to slow down and everyone else started to get up to speed with her, until the world was once again moving at a common pace. No one had seen her action; no-one had noticed her sudden movement; no one had witnessed her deliberate act of passion. The dog was sniffing at the base of a new sapling that had been planted to replace a diseased tree that was deemed hazardous. Its owner called and it obeyed straightaway, running to his side as he got up from a bench and began walking west along the south bank of the Thames towards the London Eye.

22. The Plot

Jennifer was on her way to join Harriet in Lucca. She had accepted the invitation, without any objection from Julian – who seemed pleased for her – and would be away for ten days. She had arrived in good time at the airport. With two hours at least before her departure flight, she decided to browse the best that W.H. Smith had to offer. It was a deliberate existential act to choose a paperback from the available selection. She could have pre-selected something certain but she chose to invite the hand of serendipity to offer her the necessary reading material.

She began to read the book. She knew she could do better than this effort. She knew without question that she had more wit and inventiveness at her disposal than ever the writer of this cheap thriller had. It was not arrogance on her part – it was merely a recognition of the fact. And she would prove it. Her next book would be no mere potboiler.

～

Much had occurred since that moment but her efforts were beginning to show results. She was certain now that the way to write her novel was not to outline the plot in a crystalline style, ever expanding the set of characters, their motivations, and the course of events. No. Rather it was to seek the patterns that repeated at a meta level. She had, at her fingertips, the power to imagine and to create; the power to determine and to undermine; the power to suspend her own disbelief as well as that of her diligent reader. She felt god-like in an unexpected ecstasy of creative will.

Now she must be careful. She must gather her resources, breathe deeply and regroup. There was a battle to be fought, a challenge to the divinity of her authority as author. She stopped writing and suspended action. She needed time to think.

And as she took this moment of realisation to one side and chewed upon its strings and sinews, she unwittingly allowed an opportunity for another power to enter into her unguarded imagination.

She knew that this narrative must head in a different direction now. It must become something different. It had attained a degree of self-awareness, and the characters in it too, and must now step up to a new level of expectation. The Reader who had remained faithfully with her must be rewarded for their effort - they could not be neglected or dismissed.

And then she realised: she was being watched. Someone was spying on her as she decided on a course of action, on this new direction. She would introduce them in the next chapter and they would be operating in their own secret sphere of knowledge to which she was not privy.

Whether or not this was the reality of the matter, this is what she understood it to be. Elsewhere another hand was at work; another mind imagined and controlled, at the same time as it appeared to relinquish that control to Jennifer and her characters.

～

Jennifer was elated that she had been able not only to anticipate the move by MI5 – by whoever it was – to undermine her narrative, but also to divert it and use it to her own purpose. It was this hint of hubris, unintended but present nonetheless, that was her undoing. But it would not be at the hands of those government guardians, those doers of dirty work that seek to protect our nation and preserve our way of life. No, it would be another, unexpected source – one much closer to home - an intelligence at least equal to hers, though significantly different, would establish the nature of the crime and the identity of the criminal. And this intelligence would attempt to outwit even that of the unidentified Author, the self-appointed omnipotence that sought to prevail.

Clearly the original plot, such as it was, was now in need of major revision. Matters seemed to have taken themselves out of her hands and into their own. She felt as if she were witnessing the birth of a parallel and familiar world, in which parameters were slightly shifted from those she was implicitly familiar with. The plot. How was she to resolve matters?

She had already considered doing away with a formal revelation of identity – that is to say the naming of the perpetrator or perpetrators, and a tying up of all the loose ends in a manner to satisfy all reasonable curiosity. Nevertheless she must conform to this convention, to some degree at least.

But the plot was starting to unravel before her eyes, and she felt she must be responsible. It had never been planned out in detail but she had always adhered to the conventions of the genre in all of her previous books. Somehow this was no longer the case; with this particular book she had taken a new departure. Quite unexpectedly, and without any warning, she found herself embroiled in a field of paradox and improbability. She neither knew exactly how she had arrived in this place, nor how she might extricate herself from it.

She needed some stability; she would return to her detective. He was expected to solve the mystery. If this was a whodunit then he was the archetypal nemesis, a collector of evidence and a revealer of truth. She must employ him in character. It was her duty – as a writer – it was her duty to her readers.

But another implicit presence moved to disagree. Whether or not she would learn of this other presence, in time, very much depended upon the actions, and the discoveries, of her detective, of her husband, of Inspector Julian Erasmus.

In another story he might have been the writer, and she the detective. But that would have been a different story, not this one.

23. The Harrowing

Erasmus moved into action. His existential contemplation was complete and his instincts were now given full rein. He knew exactly how he must act and what he must do. If he were to serve justice in the matter of these deaths then he must plunge into the darkness and cast light. He must become a cipher; he must return to his role as formal detective; he must solve the case.

That Robert Marston was an agent of a branch of the UK secret services was more than probable. That he had been involved in duties that led him to an untimely end was clear. Who he really was, and what his specific role was, remained uncertain.

That the boy Sam was involved in some way with the explosion and deaths at the fracking exploration site was also highly probable. The precise manner of his death was less well understood at this point in time. That there may be a link between these deaths was, currently, only speculation.

He called his team together. They met in the *Blue Anchor* overlooking the brackish waters of Chichester Harbour. The road to the pub ran along the coast between the shingle beach and the marshes, set on a raised embankment affording excellent views inland and out to sea. There were a few locals but no one to overhear their discussion of the case.

They placed their cards on the table, regarding the facts of the case. Inspector Erasmus had already called Wetherton at the Met. He had news for them. It confirmed that the Marstons were in fact a fiction. The house he had visited was empty, with no sign of recent occupancy. In the kitchen were a packet of tea bags and a carton of semi-skimmed milk, now going off. Upstairs there were signs that a table and chair had been removed.

In a corner of the front room upstairs was a crumpled receipt, from the nearby Tesco Metro, for sandwiches and a can of Coca-Cola.

Butterdale and WPC Wright had interviewed all the people at the Mournley Woods protest camp. They had not been allowed access to the exploration site but it was known that two workers had been killed in the explosion and another remained injured but stable in hospital. They concluded as follows.

Sam was known to the Camp. A young woman called Treena had been their self-elected leader, but she had disappeared and not been seen since the day before the blast occurred. Among the occasional visitors to the Camp had been a couple of young men, possibly from East Africa. They had not been seen for more than a week now but had previously been regular visitors.

Butterdale had trawled the local paper for any photographs of the camp and the protestors. He had managed to identify a woman known only as Treena and was currently running her picture online against known activist records. Inspector Erasmus thought she looked somehow familiar but he could not be certain.

WPC Wright had spoken to several of Sam's friends and his boss at the suppliers where he had worked. His recent behaviour had been uncharacteristically erratic – late for work, mind on other things, distracted – and his mother had remarked that he had missed several meals.

Erasmus sat and mused: elbows on desk, fingertips together in an arch that touched the bottom of his chin. He closed his eyes in order to see. He saw what was not to be seen: a motive for Marston's murder; a link to the death of Sam Grainger; the clandestine operations of those operating outside the law and in defence of the realm; the fanaticism of those who wanted the world to be made in their image. He drifted purposefully in this sea of, as yet, unconnected and dissonant realities.

Butterdale brought him back to the present with a start, spilling tea on the desk in front of him and splashing the Inspector's yellow silk tie – a present from his Jennifer she had bought in Florence the previous summer. Butterdale was mortified and stood aghast for a moment in stupefied silence.

"Don't worry!" said Erasmus, "No harm done. I can drop it off at the dry cleaners on my way home."

~

Inspector Erasmus sat in his favourite armchair in the snug at home. He had been listening to a quick-fire panel game on the radio – what his parents used to call the *wireless*. Of course that had a different meaning nowadays: everybody relied on wireless connectivity for their laptops and their smartphones. They were still using BlackBerry at the office. He had to admit the device was useful, if occasionally intrusive. You just had to know how to manage your accessibility. He had had to learn to use it to his advantage rather than to allow it to dictate to him. He would only check emails in the mornings before he went to work, just so that he had an idea what to expect. He did not check in the evenings; that was his own time, down time.

He had allowed his mind to wander into work territory – something he endeavoured not to do unless it were deliberate. The focus of the investigation remained, ostensibly, on the death of Sam Grainger, but despite the exclusion of other deaths, Erasmus held all evidence afloat in a sea of enquiry. The waves of thought washed upon the shores of uncertainty . . .

And into his exploration drifted the face of his wife. She was speaking to him but he could not hear what she was saying. And then he saw her at her writing desk and it was night. She wrote by the light of a brass anglepoise lamp, fitted with an old tungsten bulb that emitted yellow light. She seemed unaware and innocent of the undercurrents running through her narrative, of the clandestine activities of the secret service and the curiosity of her fictional detective-cum-husband.

Next he saw that they were together in India, visiting the Khajuraho temples, with their ancient, exotic and erotic carvings. He had felt slightly embarrassed but she had merely laughed – not out of nervousness but out of delight at the joy they expressed.

He woke with a start – his book had fallen off his knees and onto the floor. He bent down to pick up the biography of Shelley that he had bought his wife the previous Christmas. He opened the pages at random and was in Italy and the tale of Frankenstein was about to be recovered from a dream. He remembered the dreadful pursuit across the icy wastes of the Arctic, the terrible hunting of the malevolent monster by its creator. He felt the bitter cold chill the marrow of his bones.

He needed to think. He got up from his armchair and put on his coat and hat. He had a range of headgear for all weathers but on this occasion he selected one rarely worn: it was a brimless sheepskin cap that sat comfortably over his ears and kept them warm.

As he walked along the canal embankment he began to arrange what was known to him into sets of information. He would then arrange those sets alongside each other to create links. He would then refer to this picture as if he were trying to solve an anagram, shuffling the pieces into different positions and juxtapositions. What did he know and what did he *not* know?

He knew that Robert Marston had been murdered. He knew that he was of significant interest to security – probably as a courier, possibly as an informant too. He knew the manner of death. He also knew that the scene of crime had been tampered with. The curious odour, he had confirmed with forensics, was indicative of a specific cleaning agent used in embalming and the grease on the body's chin was also from the undertaker's palette . He did not know who had murdered him or why.

He knew that a bomb had been detonated at the exploration site. He knew that a young man had been found dead at the base of a chalk pit. There had been no signs of a struggle but equally nothing to indicate he had meant to take his own life. It could simply have been an accident.

(But he did not move on to considering what he did not *know. Not yet. I allowed him to forget to do so. At this time he did not know who I was, or that I existed, even if he might have suspected it.)*

He returned to the case. Butterdale had provided some information about the young woman at the protest camp who had since mysteriously vanished. Perhaps there was more grist for the mill here?

Had there been any progress on identifying the explosives used and their likely source? Again, check with Butterdale.

Something was missing. He could not see the link. He was unable to read the other parts of the story – those in which he did not appear – though he was aware of his wife's communication with her best friend, occasionally overhearing snippets of their conversations.

A moorhen splashed across the water, craking loudly, and hid itself in the reeds over by the opposite bank. He looked up and saw how far he had come. The light was fading and he turned around and marched briskly back along the towpath.

After dinner, he returned to the biography of Shelley.

The next morning he was up early. After a cup of tea and slice of toast and marmalade for breakfast (oh for a feast of bacon and eggs! But his expanding waistline warned against such folly) he washed up the plates and the knives and forks left from the night before. He was well domesticated and was quite able to look after himself in that regard. He sometimes wondered if this was because he was a modern man or, equally likely, that he was an old-fashioned self-sufficient man, used to travel and adventure, used to outdoor living, and used to fending for himself.

∼

Butterdale stumbled into the office, looking somewhat the worse for wear. His shirt was crumpled and his hair uncombed.

"Out on a blower last night, were we?" enquired the Inspector.

"No, Sir. On a *stakeout*, over Mournley way."

"Ah, I see. What did you discover?"

"More than we expected – a lot more!"

"Right. Sit down and tell me about it. I'll get some coffee."

Butterdale was clearly excited and tired at the same time. He was running on adrenaline.

Erasmus noticed a sharp sound, like the persistent cry of some electrical device, assaulting his ears. He tried to ignore the tinnitus. He swallowed hard.

"There were three of them, Sir. Three men in a white van. They were loading something – looked like crates – heavy stuff – took two of them to carry. Thought they looked like munitions – ammunition boxes – that sort of thing."

"Slow down, son. First tell me why you were on stakeout."

"Well, Sir, we had a tip off late yesterday afternoon – after you'd gone to your meeting, Sir."

The meeting. Community Liaison – obviously an important matter. But once HR had got hold of it and thoroughly over managed and mangled things, well …

"We were told the protestors were up to something and we'd better keep an eye on 'em. But it wasn't protestors we saw. Well, Sir, – I don't know if I'm supposed to say this."

"Go ahead."

"Well, it was a group of Africans, like those Olympic long-distance runners: quite wiry looking."

"I see, so probably not IRA or PLO then. What else did you see?"

The references rather bemused Butterdale – he was not a historian at all and what to Erasmus were telling observations were, to him, simply meaningless references.

"Well Sir, we followed them – WPC Wright and myself – in our unmarked vehicle. When we got to the end of the lane, by Mournley Cross, the van was rammed by another vehicle. It happened very quickly. We were stopped by two men who approached us and pointed their guns at us. They said they were anti-terrorist security forces. The main group then dragged the men from the van and bundled them into another vehicle – a lorry or large van of some kind. We were ordered to stay put. We waited until they'd all left and then of course we went to look at the van. They had emptied it and taken the crates away. But I did find this under the driver's seat. Butterdale produced a length of wire or flex – it looked familiar.

"How's WPC Wright? Have you reported this yet?"

"She'll be fine Sir, a bit shaken up – that's all. And when the SOCOs got there, there was no sign of the van – no tyre marks, no broken glass – nothing. The incident had been 'vanished'."

"I see," said Erasmus, speaking almost to himself, as if a light was beginning to dawn somewhere in the recesses of his mind but had not yet flickered into a fully fledged flame.

⁓

He had not forgotten. He knew that his quarry still eluded him. Whoever was writing this commentary was equally aware that he, Erasmus, was getting closer to some kind of realisation. Soon they would become counter-poised in a balance of intellectual equals – each fully aware of the other; each establishing the existence of the other; each seeking to derive their own meaning from the other.

⁓

For the moment the authorial view reigned but it must soon give way to the voice of another and others, of the characters that had been created. Once Erasmus knew of the fineness of his existence, of its tenuousness in the writing and the reading? The others were blissfully ignorant, and seemingly no worse off for being so. If this makes us not a little conceited in some way, then it is hardly surprising. Of course you are also privy to this conceit, this dramatic device, but you already know that and I do not need to remind you.

24. An Ending of Sorts

The case was not so much closed, as the door was now opened. If Erasmus had identified the cause and effect, the lineage of events leading to murder, then he had also started to uncover another, far more curious set of workings. There were still only hints rather than facts but he knew he must tread carefully between the realms of fantasy and reality.

He was well aware of the standard theological problem of free will versus predestination – given his heritage, that was a certainty. Although he had not expended a great deal of thought on this particular metaphysical issue lately – or 'challenge' as HR would say nowadays, in its wholesale swallowing of all things American – nonetheless he could see it was fundamental to his quest. Had he done enough to justify his own existence, independent of external forces and directing powers? Was he being manipulated by MI5? Could he know if he had achieved a sufficient degree of independence? Was he now acting with free will, or was he acting only under the duress of some other unknown power?

There remained gaps in his knowledge of precisely who Marston was or what his role might have been. There was uncertainty about his own and others existence – but that was not fruitful, he felt, and so he chose to be as he was and to exist in the person he had become. But he now knew he had a purpose. He must continue to be aware of, and look out for, the hand that holds the pen, for the mind that drives the thought.

～

Jennifer had boarded her flight and, with the additional leg-room afforded by an upgrade to world-flyer class, had settled in for the long haul.

She let her mind relax, releasing herself from the rigours of writing, and she scanned the pages of the in-flight magazine. There was an article on pre-war flying boats and the Imperial Airways East Africa route to Cape Town. It used to take four and a half days to complete the journey then. But there were overnight stopovers in Italy and the Sudan and the experience was one of luxury and adventure combined. The trip nowadays was faster and more convenient but also far more prosaic.

She felt relieved, exhausted, excited, tearful – all these physical and emotional states in quick succession and sometimes simultaneously. She was going to meet Harriet in Nairobi and then they would make their way to Mombasa. From there they would go on to the Tsavo National Park, north-east of the city.

～

It is dark. An invisible hand places something carefully by the roadside – an old jerry-can perhaps - and walks away briskly. There are packs of feral dogs out hunting at night and it is best not to linger. The deep skies are filled with the stars of our galaxy, and beyond are those we cannot see with the naked eye, but there is no time to admire their accidental beauty.

～

It was a typically hot and humid day in Mombasa. A young woman ran to greet her guardian, Harriet, as she came through the arrivals gate at the local airport.

"Auntie Harriet! I'm so glad you came. Everything's planned. Is this all your luggage?"

They embraced, then Harriet turned and ushered forward her companion.

"Hello Katerina, do you remember me?" She did. Of course she did, but she was clearly surprised to see her. She tried not to show it more than was polite. She was in fact genuinely surprised – but this would not seriously affect her plans, it merely required a minor alteration. She would phone the Safari Lodge and tell them to make an addition to their party.

Treena led them to where their taxi was waiting to drive them on to the Lodge. They would be there about an hour after nightfall, all being well.

The group of visitors did not arrive at the Lodge that evening as expected. The rooms were made up, the beds turned down, and places were reserved for dinner. Instead they encountered an I.E.D. on the road from town to the National Park. The driver was killed instantly in the blast. It was assumed that Al Shabad had crossed over from Somalia in another, increasingly frequent, terrorist incursion.

～

Sir Lionel was in a state of shock. Somehow he had failed – he had failed to see the strength in his target, the strength that was also her flaw; he had failed to predict the unintended outcome of his plan to divert and diffuse; he had failed. But he was not finished. It was time to enter the fray. It was time to act directly.

"Ms Jenkins – a flight to Nairobi – today. Thank you."

He called Nairobi on a secure line. He told them he would be arriving the next morning.

25. Announcement

Sir Lionel Wilberforce (Bart), CBE, Colonel Royal Green Jackets (Retd.) b.1969 - d.2024 Killed in Action, Mogadishu, Somalia, attempting to rescue British hostages held by the terrorist group Al Shabad.

"No greater love hath man than that he should lay down his life for others."

The funeral service will take place at 2 p.m. on June 24th at St Egbert's Church, Marsham-on-the-Moor.
No flowers please. Donations to *Hope for Heroes*.

26. Shock

Perhaps he was still in shock. Perhaps it hadn't struck home yet. Perhaps he just didn't believe it. His wife had been killed by Al Shabad terrorists in East Africa.

He re-read the note she had left him on the kitchen table, written hastily while she waited for the taxi to take her to Gatwick Airport:

I'll only be gone a couple of weeks and there's plenty of food in the freezer. If you want something to do then have a look at my latest manuscript. I think you'll find it quite interesting – it's a bit different! There's the taxi !

Jennifer
XXX

P.S. Don't forget to feed the cat.

Unusually, they had not made love the night before she left. He understood. He did not feel sad. He was not sure what he felt.

He knew, of course, that she was going to Kenya; had been told she was going to visit her best friend Harriet; he had thought nothing of it – other than that he would have the chance to cook a curry every night, should he so choose. . Perhaps he would find things a bit quiet at first, but he would soon occupy himself cataloguing his treen collection, and perhaps adding to it with the occasional new purchase on eBay. Mrs Phillips would still be coming to do the cleaning. Secretly he was looking forward to some time to himself, in his own company.

Erasmus had been given compassionate leave – he had not wanted to take it but the Assistant Chief Constable had insisted. Now Inspector

Julian Erasmus would have to face facts and, although used to doing so in his professional life, he was less adept at doing so in his private life. He had realised that, whilst there was a huge empty hole, there was also a curious sense of relief that tilted him towards guilt. If he could not work then he must occupy himself, both his mind and his body, and even his emotions, to avoid coming to a complete halt.

He had begun by visiting his elder sister. She had relayed the news around the family. He was grateful for this. Then he had devised a plan – not a plan so much as an approach to things. He would carry out a fact-finding review of his own personal history, in order to understand how he had arrived at this point in his life. He wanted to believe it had been worthwhile. He wanted to know if he was angry, if he was sad, if he was curious – if he felt anything at all, if any of it made any sense. He would be fine as long as he had an answer, but for the moment he didn't. He decided to start at the beginning.

~

As he climbed the hill the odd and even house numbers continued to ascend in harmony till he stopped at number fort-seven. It did not seem to have changed much – even the double glazing occupied the same thirties style bay-windows and the pebble-dash was still a creamy-white colour. Perhaps he had misremembered red or green window-frames – perhaps that was the pre-Lego, Bayko building bricks, the ones he used to play with as a child. This was where it had started – his life. This is where he had been born, at home. He searched for some resonance but there was none; it was too long ago, as if it had happened to someone else.

As he turned to walk back down the hill a neighbour hailed him from behind a hedge that he was carefully trimming with hand-shears. They spoke briefly and the man recalled his family, though they had moved in only shortly before the Erasmus' had left. Erasmus declined the offer of a cup of tea but thanked the man kindly.

At the station he walked to the far end of the platform, then he stood and mused awhile, wondering what, if anything, he had discovered.

He now knew for certain that Jenny had not been the sole author of her destiny. She could not have written herself out of her own storyline – or could she? It didn't seem to make any sense. Nothing seemed to make any sense. He suspected that shock was a process and not merely an event; it was in fact a state – of mind, of being, both mental and physical, and moreover emotional. So far he had felt nothing – unless that itself were some kind of emotion?

Now he had more time on his own than he had ever expected and he wasn't sure whether or not to feel pleased about it. Of course this was unforgiveable but, to be honest, it is how he felt. He didn't know why and he couldn't explain it – it was just how it was. He was retracing his life, visiting key places and associated memories and mis-remembered memories. As he walked up the hill he glanced at the numbers on the doors – evens on the left, odds on the right. It was a typical collection of inter-war years houses – semi-detached, bay window, well-kept gardens and now every driveway held one or more cars. This was the same hill he had walked down, holding his father's hand, when he was no more than perhaps four or five. He remembered (he remembered) that sunny day quite clearly – it was almost his first memory. Quite why he found himself retracing those small steps so many years later, he was not sure. His older sister had said he would recognise the bakelite door-handles; he could recall nothing of the interior of the house – only a photograph of himself and the other children, seated or standing on an old settee. He felt a sudden wave of guilt sweep through his body like lava. He held his breath and clutched his arm. It passed. He drew some deep breaths and stood still, holding the panic at bay. This had happened once or twice before; now he recognised it.

He boarded the train back to town but could not concentrate well enough to read. He stared out of the window at the suburban sprawl, spotted with small allotments and brave attempts at gardening, and counted the villages he knew that were now unrecognisable as such – most of them had not been unlinked villages for as far back as he could remember. But he was remembering through the blood that ran in his veins, blood that seemed to inherit the years of anonymity endured by his ancestors, and now by himself.

Suddenly the train lurched forward and he was almost flung off his seat. Fortunately there was no-one sitting opposite so no need to offer anyone an apology. He sat back again and closed his eyes. All too soon they had arrived at the terminus. He got off the train – waiting in a queue for the exit, wishing they still had the old slam-door trains - and walked to the barriers. His mobile rang. He answered it. It was D.S. Butterdale.

"Sorry to bother you Sir, I know you're off duty, but you said to call you if we had any news at all."

"That's okay. Go ahead."

Butterdale was as succinct as possible, trying to keep to the point as he had been taught.

"Evans has told us to see him at tomorrow morning, ten o'clock sharp. He's coming to the office."

"Is he expecting me too?"

"Didn't say, Sir."

"Not to worry. Thanks for letting me know. Just answer his questions – no more and no less – you know the routine."

"Will you be there, Sir?"

"No, I don't think so. I'm sure you can handle it."

So saying he ended the call and resumed his approach to the ticket barrier. He had other business to attend to - Evans could wait!

27. Home

Erasmus arrived home about twenty minutes later, after a brisk walk from the station. He took his keys from his inside pocket and opened the front door. A cat rubbed against his legs. He had forgotten they had a cat but it was seeking affection or, more likely, wishing to be fed. Erasmus took his coat off, went into the kitchen and opened a cupboard, hoping it would be the correct cupboard – it was. He did not know that he had known where to find the cat food until he realised he had opened the correct cupboard without even thinking about it. He was beginning to realise the benefit of his ability to move to the outside and look in on actions and events. It was an experience akin to those who, lying on the operating table, look down upon themselves from above, he imagined. Jenny had once described this phenomenon to him.

Erasmus wished he could ignore the cat. He was a reminder. He made him think of his immediate past and his previous domestic comfort, and he reminded him of the hollowness of his life. He provided a continuance that he would prefer did not exist. This informed his approach to his work. He wanted to concentrate on the present, on the nuances that informed his investigation, and not be distracted by what had happened in the past. He wanted to exploit this new-found freedom to devote all his attention to the case, now that he had no marital or domestic responsibilities to concern him.

Erasmus' cat was called Cheshire. When a human called him, it was not simply the tone of voice that caught his attention. He was an intelligent cat. A cat's intelligence is not a human intelligence, of course.
It knows reality in the context of its own terms of reference. A cat prowls and patrols; a cat purrs and prefers; a cat pounces and plays. It does all these things by instinct but learns to develop them by intent. A cat

responds to its human servants only as it suits, and then no more.

Cheshire was a pitch-black cat. He had been with the Erasmus from a very early age, having been rescued from a sack thrown into the canal. Cheshire knew he was a cat and he knew he was in charge. Humans were merely useful. He had no knowledge of their motives and intentions but he was very familiar with their daily routines. Their toilet was no more private than if it had been conducted in an amphitheatre or displayed on a wide-screen in 3D at the cinema. He was neither a voyeur nor a prude and considered himself to be merely an observer of the human condition in its physical aspect. He noted that humans were noisy in their love-making and careless with their offspring. He would often lie comfortably on a baby asleep in its pram, where it had been placed in the fresh air for its health. Sometimes he would cover its face till it wriggled and squawked and became an uncomfortable cushion; then he would jump down and go for a stroll, in search of mice or voles to play with. Sometimes he would find a chick fallen from its nest – but this was no challenge. He preferred the game he could play with a slow-worm or a lizard. He had been surprised at the reptiles' ability to shed their tails, but then he had tried to induce this response in his playmates – it amused him.

He had established a territory and he defended it vigorously. It extended as far as the church fields on one side and the canal on the other; it covered the full extent of the Close north to south. Recently he had followed Erasmus as far as the canal – he wanted him to take him with him. He had ambitions to extend his territory. Erasmus had discouraged him. He did not want to be followed into town.

And of course Cheshire knew that, as well as one or two other things that he would never have admitted, had he been asked.

"Cheshire!" Erasmus called the cat for dinner. Cheshire appeared almost immediately, as if out of nowhere.

"Ah there you are. What have you been up to then? I don't suppose you've been writing up endless reports, have you?"

When Erasmus talked to the cat he was talking partly to himself. Cheshire knew that a human liked to make these sounds just as he like to purr and *miaow*.

Cheshire seemed to smile at Erasmus as he prepared his dinner, and rubbed against his legs, purring loudly. He knew he was in danger of being (gently) kicked away but he could not resist the temptation to express his devoted cupboard-love. When dinner was served, Cheshire would consider it for a short while and then begin to pick delicately at this long-awaited feast, as if dining only out of social obligation.

Sometimes Cheshire would vacate his usual home and take up residence elsewhere for a while. Usually he found a lonely old lady or made friends, temporarily, with another cat, sharing its food in unequal portions. Sometimes he would not be seen for a week or more. Then, for no particular reason – a whim perhaps – he would reappear. Then Erasmus would once again remember he owned a cat.

When he had finished the washing-up, Erasmus switched on the television. It was time for the news. A man had been seen waving an ISAL flag in Parliament Square. The police questioned the man but no arrest was made. Erasmus wondered, he wondered what constituted incitement, and he wondered if free speech was sacrosanct. Cheshire rubbed against his legs and Erasmus picked him up and sat him on his lap. The cat purred contentedly and dug his claws into his thighs, as if he knew more than anyone else might suspect.

It was difficult for Erasmus to say exactly when he had rejected his heritage, intellectually. Emotionally and temperamentally he knew aspects would remain with him for his whole life. His thinking had been influenced, whilst at University, by various contemporary writers and philosophers but mostly by his interest in scientific method. He was not a poetical man and although his wife had tried to interest him in poets and poetry he much preferred prose. He was for fact over fiction. This was not to say he had no imagination – far from it. He was able to read characters, their motivations and their intentions, without a training in Conrad, Meredith, or James. He knew he preferred to stand on the outside, looking in. He understood that he was neither left nor right in his politics, though neither was he neutral. He was a product of Western culture, that curious admixture of Christian tradition and the Enlightenment, as well as the embodiment of a seemingly unbroken family tradition that pointed back to a line of upright, but anonymous, ancestors. He had always been curious about his surname. He suspected it might have been adopted, in deference to the great Renaissance Humanist of the same name. Such an idea further supported his Huguenot theory. He hoped he had 'inherited' his worldly wisdom to some degree.

Erasmus took a bottle of his favourite malt from the back of the drinks-cabinet. He scooped a cluster of ice cubes from the cold bucket. The sintered ice formed a pyramid-like structure at the bottom of the glass. He picked up Jennifer's incomplete manuscript and began to read. The working title was 'Fractal'. He read continuously and finished it in one sitting. He was both amused and astonished, in equal measure. This was certainly different from Jennifer's run-of-the-mill efforts. He now knew that his wife had written him into the plot and that his role was to solve the murders. He knew that she was conscious that matters had got out of hand. He suspected she was aware of MI5's involvement – or whoever it might be misleading them – he realised she had been aware of another hand at work in proceedings, one that led him to feel an increasing sense of foreboding.

∼

Erasmus felt that he must satisfy not only his own professional curiosity, but that of the honest Reader also. He realised that the attempt of the writer, his wife Jennifer, to create a multi-layered landscape in which control evolved and devolved to more than a single character or action, was itself a liberty – an indulgence that not everyone would be willing to accept. The Reader might perhaps decide that they could write a better thriller and return this one to W.H. Smiths at the airport on their return.

He turned his attention to the matter in hand. His wife had revealed that 'he' was the main character in her latest book. There was a hint – more than a hint – that he was to play a vitally important role in the whole business, and that it was one that was beyond solving the usual murders of any middle-of-the-road detective story. He tried to summarise matters; he tried to understand exactly how he was placed at this juncture: the events that had taken place so far were of her own invention, himself included. And yet, if that were the case, was she not also a character in her own fiction, was she not also a creation of her own imagination? was it in fact too reflexive for apprehension, or for intellectual understanding, as opposed to intuition? Perhaps it would be best, for the time being, to take things at face value. He returned to the matter in hand – the murder and the deaths in the explosion, and that of a young man nearby. He at least knew that this was no time to be self-indulgent or engage in ironic playfulness – he had his duty.

Erasmus knew he was marking time. The plot must hasten on. The Reader must be enticed, then captured, then held until the end of the story. He felt that, in his wife's absence, he must play the role of Master of Ceremonies. He would need all his skill and experience to follow not only the likely twists and turns of a writer's imagination – he must also divine the workings of the invisible hand beyond his wife's imagination. He must do these things in order not merely to assert his own identity but also, and more importantly, to confirm its independence. For him it had become a matter of existential importance. He would descend into the shades and he would seek there the specific answers, the undiscovered meanings, and the solutions to the patchwork narrative in which all this is woven.

He had reached a conclusion – it was tentative and still needed a further degree of proof – but it was more than a working hypothesis. It satisfied the facts and it satisfied reasonable curiosity. It only remained to test it against the reality that had been constructed, stated, and implied in all that had gone before, with minimal addition of further information not already deducible or consistent with the known facts of the case. He would need to apply Occam's Razor with clinical precision. He swilled the mixture in the bottom of his glass, the last drop of malt swirling round the icy rocks. He finished his drink and mulled as the warm glow faded. Everything was caste in a new light. He needed time to take it all in.

He got up, put his old coat on, and went out for a walk.

28. Cathedral

It was Wednesday and Erasmus was not due back at work until the following Monday. He had time to think. He felt a tinge of guilt. He had always been too busy, it seemed, to accompany Jennifer up to town, to the Tate Britain or the Tate Modern, for the latest major exhibition. Now he was here at the Pallant House Gallery, off South Street, in the middle of Chichester, examining an exhibition of paintings, by British painters, from the First and Second World Wars. He had simply been wandering, with no particular purpose or destination in mind, and found himself outside the Gallery. He entered. He had a coffee in the café. He browsed for a long time in the bookshop, but bought nothing, not even a postcard. And when he had finished failing to occupy his mind, or to dispel the invading thoughts that entered his mind unbidden from each and every direction, he left the gallery, weaving his away along the narrow streets until he reached the cathedral.

He needed time to digest everything and form his strategy. He needed an overall purpose and some short-term aims that would get him closer to achieving his goal. To do this he would firstly take stock of his own personal and professional history. He needed to know where he had taken a wrong path, if indeed he had. He needed to understand himself, beyond what he thought he already knew.

Erasmus seated himself at the rear of the Cathedral. It was a spacious building, well-lit. Famous for its spire, that could be seen for miles around, he also enjoyed the John Piper altarpiece – very much of its time in the late 1950's and early '60's. It was bold and angular and colourful. It was modern. He felt comfortable in this space. It was welcoming and left him to himself, if he so wished. Here he could sit. He could think or not think, just as he chose. Sometimes it was good simply to be, to be both empty of thoughts and not at all over-awed, at one and the same time. This was the perfect place for this unintended purpose. It was something that one had to slip into, almost accidentally and without conscious effort, in order to appreciate its full and priceless blessing.

On this occasion, late on a Saturday afternoon, the orchestra and soloists were running through sections of Handel's *Messiah*. Erasmus felt both privileged to be present at this impromptu performance and, at the same time, not a little proud that he too had sung in a choir, whilst at college, this very same magnificent piece. Though even then he had not worn a bow tie.

Jennifer used to mock him mildly about his rather dull and puritan dress sense, but he didn't really mind. She loved clothes and he had learnt something from her about their worth and value. They really did make a difference to one's performance in public, to the way in which you were perceived, the way in which people treated you, and also how you felt about yourself, often making you more confident. However, he knew he had to draw the line at some point and for him, by heritage and temperament, it was definitely before he ever got near a bow tie. He chuckled silently to himself. He really must take his winter coat to the dry cleaners. And he would look at buying a new stylish Italian leather jacket.

Erasmus sat still, breathing gently, almost as if in a contemplative trance. He was piecing together the elements – the half hints and misleading clues – in an effort to sift the assorted red herrings from the sheep and goats, and to contrive a unity of events, an explanation that would conform to the normal basis of reality. He knew – of course he knew – that there is always more to things than meets the eye. He knew all was not as it seemed. He knew it was his job, regardless, to bring a focus to bear that would solve the problem; not only the murders, but the problem, as it now stood, and as he strongly suspected he had not yet fully appreciated.

He had been sure of himself. Very sure of himself. It had taken him a long time to rid himself of his natural predisposition to assume the good in men, despite a huge helping of original sin in his daily diet as a young man. He always preferred to give the benefit of the doubt, and to assume the best – or at least, not the worst. This inherited cultural and religious naivety he had gradually sloughed, like an ill-fitting suit, until he was now able to place himself in a variety of positions and standpoints; he was now able to view things in the round, knowing which assumptions he might be making, and understand which facts he might be selecting at the expense of others. He had cultivated a healthy degree of suspicion. In this way he was no less sure of himself, but he was far more effective at his job.

He reflected on this description of himself: was it accurate? Was there at least a degree of truth in it? Would he say this of himself? Who might describe him thus? It was not inaccurate by any means, but these were not the words he would choose. And yet he had selected them.

As a postmodern non-conformist – in the sense that he had rejected his formal theological upbringing but retained its essentially individualistic disposition – Julian Erasmus was not liable to let things drift or disregard his duty. Rather he was inclined to pay heed to matters with a scrupulousness born out of habit. He inclined to the ethical position, regardless, and took the side of the weak against the strong as a matter of innate disposition. All in all he was a good man and would not be damned, despite himself. He had learnt to apportion his time and his thoughts according to the needs of the day or the matter in hand. He had learnt when to take control and when to let go. He had learnt to be himself and to be comfortable with who he was. He had no unnecessary sense of guilt – he had forgiven himself for all he had done and would forgive himself his mistakes in the future. He was sufficiently self-aware to be happy in his skin and certain of nothing except the need to maintain an order of justice. This was his chosen life and gave him meaning.

Erasmus noticed that his thoughts had sped off on an unintended tangent but he allowed them to continue to their own natural conclusion.

There was a suspicion – never substantiated with evidence, other than that provided by oral tradition - that his family were originally Huguenots, come over from the Lowlands in the Puritan purges of the Seventeenth Century. That may indeed have been the case, but he was unlikely to be able to find documentary evidence, even though Census data was now generally available on line as far back as 1861. One day, perhaps when he was retired, with time on his hands, he would trace his roots more precisely. However he had arrived at this time and place, in the middle of this investigation, he knew exactly where he stood with himself and with the world at large.

But it was not just that. If it were, it would be merely a case of applying his professional skills to the abstract problem. At this point in time he needed to play his part within, and distinct from, the intentions of those who controlled his thoughts and actions. He must become self-realised and fully independent. His instantiation as an authorial actor in this piece of writing was paramount. He drew on the self–sufficiency of his non-conformist upbringing to provide him with the strength and stamina he needed. This was absolutely fundamental: it was a matter of his own individual autonomy. He must prove his ability to become and to be. He must bring himself into existence.

I had assumed the story was at an end, but it seems the characters thought otherwise. With the nominal Writer killed off I had assumed I would be free to write – or not to write – as I saw fit. But it was not to be. The story seemed to have a life of its own and I was now in thrall to it, without freedom to resist beyond an occasional reflection, such as this. If this were the game then I'd better play it well; there is no other to do this work. I feel the presence of Inspector Erasmus, as if he were only a few steps behind me; I need to increase the distance between us.

All things were drawing to a precise point, a single moment, an irreversible decision. Erasmus had moved himself carefully into position, on the outside looking in. From here he began to see things more clearly – no longer through a glass darkly. He felt he was starting to assume control, not only of the plot but also of himself as an autonomous, active and effecting agent in the fiction, and beyond.

～

Erasmus sensed that the narrative might now be pliable to his own will and invention. It was as if he had taken up the pen his wife had left behind and, as a debt of honour, he was now starting to become a creator of actions and events. He had begun his pursuit of the truth on one level of understanding, but he was now shifting to another. It was no longer merely a murderer he sought, it was an alter ego, an opaque presence, an invisible hand.

It was a moment of calm but irrevocable revelation.

29. Interlude

It was as yet unclear whether to continue or not. Reception of the first part needed to be gauged. Then, and only then, would it be known if it was worth continuing with the story, or not. Patience was required. In the meantime thoughts must be gathered as they arrived, and filed for future reference. If it was necessary to mark time then it was equally necessary not to waste it. Hedge the future, sell the past. A useful motto.

~

He knew that Erasmus was onto him. He knew that his position was unsafe. He knew he must tread carefully. What he had not reckoned on was Erasmus' stamina and tenacity, together with his willingness to recreate himself. He had known from the outset he would prove a strong character but he had not reckoned on this. Of all the characters in the story this was the one that had assumed a life of its own and would not easily be disposed of. His wife had been a simple matter – there was nothing to be gained in keeping her. Harriet's destiny was less certain; she had been more interesting and less predictable. The minor characters merely served their purpose. It was Erasmus who was proving to be a headache, and more than a match for him.

For the moment he would mark time. For now it was a waiting game and - patience was required. Perhaps something else to occupy mind and body? Perhaps a walk by the sea or a recuperative mountain holiday in Switzerland would do the trick?

It was no good. The thing had developed a momentum all of its own and seemed to insist on being written. Already this element of choice had been relinquished – what would be next? What tactic might he employ to regain some degree of control?

Perhaps he could introduce a substitute Author – someone already in the frame. What about Jennifer's sister? What if Raffington hadn't drowned in the Thames? What if MI5 had actually succeeded and were now pulling the strings? The idea was considered, then rejected. He would return to Erasmus' self-analysis, his autobiographical sojourn, gathering in and sifting the debris of his life. This would occupy his time and energy; this would hold him at bay.

He turned to Erasmus, Inspector Erasmus, so fortuitously promoted and hurled into the fray by his now departed wife.

He reflected on his choices. Erasmus remained unaware of the part the Colonel had played in the fate of his wife, and this must remain so, under the terms of the Official Secrets Act. Where had he left Inspector Erasmus? Was it at Waterloo or Victoria Station? For a moment he couldn't remember. He searched back through the previous pages.

Erasmus was in fact, just then, studying the departure timetable at Liverpool Street Station. He was on his way to Cambridge, a city he hadn't visited for a very long time, not since his undergraduate days as an occasional visitor down from London for the weekend.

30. Jigsaw

WPC Wright's secondment had been extended indefinitely. The Assistant Chief Constable had sufficient observational skills of his own to realise that the team of three was starting to gel and deliver. He had never doubted Erasmus' natural ability, nor his dedication, but he wanted to take things to the next level. He trusted in his own judgement with only the slightest twinge of doubt – was he going out on a limb? He consoled himself with a scrap of positive thinking gleaned, not from a training course for senior officers, but from his own grandmother. The Assistant Chief Constable had a record of his grandmother's sayings, written down in a little notebook, which he kept on the mantelpiece behind the clock. He would look at it every so often and try to identify which ones were from old music hall songs, or others that could be catchphrases from programs on the wireless, or perhaps handed down the generations by familial oral tradition. For the moment he invoked a favourite of her sayings: "Nothing ventured, nothing gained!"

﹏

Evans was cold, matter of fact, and precise. There was no unnecessary social interaction. He implicitly assumed that intimidation was the way to deliver results. His ability to do so was only matched by his inability to understand the limitations of this approach. He began his first interview of the day:

"D.S. Butterdale?"

"Yes, Sir."

"What can you tell me about Sam Grainger?"

"Well Sir, not much I'm afraid. Young man. Usual idealism. Lived at home with his mother. Tragic accident by the looks of it. Tumbled from the top of the chalk pit – broke his neck."

"Did you consider it might have been anything other than an accident?"

"Well if it was, we found no evidence to that effect."

Butterdale knew he was treading dangerous waters. Best stick to the truth, or as close to, and not invent anything. At the same time he would not offer anything unless asked.

"What about indications of anyone else having been in the vicinity?"

"Well Sir, we did find evidence that people had been smoking dope up there, but there was nothing in the lad's system, according to the autopsy."

He realised he had said more than he meant to.

"And did you establish who else might have used the chalk pit for this purpose? Did you in fact try to find out?"

"Well, we interviewed all the protestors at the camp and they certainly knew Sam Grainger – I mean, they'd seen him around – but other than that no, not really."

"I see. That's all for now." Send in WPC Wright on your way out, would you?"

Butterdale felt hot and flushed. The back of his hands itched and his throat was dry. He was glad to get out of the interview room. Evans must know – or at least suspect – they had a lead. Could there have been some connection to the bombing at the exploration site?

Evans remained inscrutable as he quizzed WPC Wright in a similar fashion – only she was not flustered at all and remained calm and co-operative whilst managing to say nothing at all of any consequence. He knew he was being played – felt it in his bones – but could not pin down anything specific that made him think this. He made a mental note to speak to the Evaluation Team – this woman could be an excellent recruit.

Erasmus was not unduly concerned at Evans' reappearance but he wanted to be kept informed of his moves nonetheless. It was best never to underestimate the opposition, even if you were supposedly on the same side – especially if you were on the same side.

He was on his way to Cambridge. As a pretentious grammar school boy he had never entertained any thoughts of going either to Oxford or Cambridge. Instead he had plumped for a selection of colleges in London and had been accepted by one that did not require him to sit an entrance examination, but accepted his extant examination results. He had enjoyed his time as an undergraduate, taking full advantage of the theatres, museums, and art galleries scattered so generously throughout the capital. He had visited Thomas Carlyle's house in Chelsea, and watched Sir Alec Guinness perform his one man show depicting the life of Jonathan Swift. He had watched the boat race from a flat in Chiswick and had been to see *England v Scotland* at Twickenham. Occasionally he had been to visit friends studying in Cambridge. On one occasion he met his old Classics master, outside Kings College Chapel, and they had exchanged Latin salutations.

Was there some other unfinished business there that gnawed away at the back of his mind and insisted he return to it? What had he forgotten? The facts were known, but the emotional turmoil had been lost along the way, misplaced or deliberately hidden. It was a dangerous time to revisit and he could do so only obliquely, but he must do so; it was necessary to establish his own existence.

There followed a sequence of places and times that included his original British Council posting to Paris, and then Berlin, followed by a troubled time in the Middle East. On returning to England he had discovered a strange anger within himself that was the result of reverse culture shock. He had, for several years now, forgotten most of this but occasional snippets had started to come at him, with increasing frequency and from unexpected angles. Shaving one morning, he had remembered the migrating birds that stopped over for a few days on the building site opposite his third floor flat. He could think of nothing in particular that should have brought this to mind.

Gradually Erasmus was beginning to piece things together; his conscious effort to revisit and reconcile the elements of his past was beginning to bear fruit. But he still needed to cross-reference the experiences and the feelings he had suffered or enjoyed. His late wife might have been able to do so in part but there was much unknown even to her. He had deliberately kept much from her, more to protect himself than her, he now realised.

He noticed his observations were devoid of feeling: no pang of guilt, no sudden flash of sorrow, no numbness, just an absence of – what exactly?

∼

All the while Erasmus was falling further behind as he continued to assert his own identity. This was an opportunity to create more distance. I was right: it had not been necessary to introduce another author-character. In fact, I shall allow Erasmus to create this narrative, stepping back to watch as he does so. I am rather beginning to enjoy myself, I must admit.

∼

It seemed obvious to Inspector Erasmus that the security services were keen to know more about the mysterious Treena. His own team's researches had turned up little more than that she had been engaged in various protest marches – all legitimate and non-violent. Nevertheless he had a suspicion. Was she actually an *agent provocateur* of the state? Might she have been playing a double-game? Or was it simply that she was more involved, more directly involved, in the bombing of the fracking site, and she was some sort of eco-terrorist? And why did she seem oddly familiar?

It was time for Erasmus to get his affairs in order at home. The unsettling and protracted business of obtaining probate, even with the 'assistance' of a solicitor as executor, was wearing. Then there were the constant reminders of his wife: her wardrobe, photographs, herbal teas in the cupboard next to fridge, shoes in the cupboard under the stairs. He called her sister Becky and asked her to come over at the weekend. His wife's memorial service had been held a month previously and it was no longer premature to think of getting rid of her remaining things.

Becky was upset by her younger sister's death but retained, in public, a deliberate demeanour of self-control that belied any emotion or display of grief. She knew what needed to be done and was prepared to do it. She collected some jewellery and other keepsakes left to her in Jennifer's will, but her clothes were carefully folded and parcelled up in vacuum pack bags with anti-moth sachets; these bags would be donated to a charity for refugees. Jennifer's library: her travel guides and cookery books, her romantic poetry collection and her own novels was more problematic. Julian decided to keep the novels, though actually he had only read the first one fully – the others he had merely skimmed.

Becky asked about photograph albums: were there any containing pictures from their childhood? Julian went to the snug and found them on the shelves behind the armchair. He carried them back through to the living room. They started to skim through them to identify the albums with pictures from his wife's life before they met. He recognised Becky, and Jennifer's best friend Harriet. Then there were some pictures of holidays the two of them had taken together – an early one somewhere up in the Lake District – two attractive young girls in their early twenties perhaps.

"I think this is the one you want, Becky."

She took it and looked at the black and white photographs – always so fresh and timeless, as if taken only yesterday, and more vital than the instant digital colour photos we have nowadays. Julian looked over her shoulder as she flicked through the pages, stopping occasionally to reminisce.

"Wait a minute – just go back a page. Who's that girl with Jennifer and Harriet?"

"I think it's Harriet's niece – well her ward really – yes, her name's Katerina, if I remember rightly. I met her just the once but that must be about ten years ago now. I dropped Jennifer off in town – she was going shopping with Harriet - and she had Katerina with her for the day.

Erasmus looked carefully at the photograph. He couldn't be sure but he strongly suspected – there was a definite likeness to the young woman at the protestors' camp in Mournley Woods. It was not that he didn't believe in coincidences, but neither did he like them.

He helped Becky load the car with the items they had sorted to dispose of. It felt unfair but honest – Jennifer would not have expected sentimentality; nor would she have approved of it. She would have seen the practical sense in what they were doing now. Life moves on.

"Here," said Becky, "they're from the garden – Victoria plums. I know you like them."

"Yes, yes I do. Thank you. I'll have some for dinner."

It was a small gesture which might have seemed pathetic to some, but to Erasmus it was a statement of all that remained unsaid between them, and for Becky it was all she had to offer. She assumed he must be devastated; he assumed she had never been close to his wife, her sister. He felt nothing; she felt puzzled, as if none of it made any sense. He waved as she drove off, and again as she turned the corner, and then he lost sight of the car. He turned to go back indoors, into a familiar but empty house. The emptiness of the house seemed to balance his own emotional hollowness, as if the outer and inner worlds of experience were poised in perfect disharmony.

31. Strategy

Everyone has their own strategy for doing jigsaw puzzles. Most start
by searching the pieces for all the straight edges. The corner pieces -
those that provide the overall frame of reference - are most prized of all.
Erasmus also employed a standard strategy when dealing with puzzles for
which he only had some of the pieces, and it was not dissimilar. The initial
problem he faced was that there was no picture to follow and the corners
could not immediately be placed in their correct positions.

Erasmus needed a strategy for this particular puzzle, in which he was
inextricably involved. To date this had been to consolidate and review, to
re-establish himself. To achieve this he had sought to rediscover, or at
least revisit, significant times and places in search of – well, to see what
might happen. He felt that this approach would at least bring a change,
and that was what he needed now and what he intended. He was adrift,
ranging far and wide, in what was potentially both a fruitful and a
dangerous enterprise. He must operate on two levels and in two spheres:
the first clearly literal and professional, and also at the meta-level, which
challenged his very existence.

If he were to succeed, he first needed to isolate the two main parts of
the puzzle. If he concentrated on the standard investigation initially, he
might learn to deal with the other obliquely. He decided to devote his
conscious attention to the work of his team and the quizzing that Evans
had, for some as yet unknown reason, found necessary to conduct. He
called Wetherton at the Met.

Wetherton was free the following evening and they arranged to meet
in a pub called *The Hole in the Wall* near London Bridge. Erasmus was
about an hour early for their appointment and decided to walk back
across the bridge, leaving the Shard behind on his right, towards the City.

The late workers were leaving their offices and straggling home, just in time to turn around and come back again the next day. Eliot's recasting of Dante's line came to him unbidden – 'I did not think death had undone so many' – and he remembered a visit he had made to Little Gidding with a group of University students. But he had no picture of the place, no memory of the deep discussions or the particular purpose of the retreat. Some things are remembered with curious and startling accuracy, whilst others seem almost a blank. On reaching the far end of the bridge he stood awhile, then turned around and walked back again, halting in the middle of the bridge to look east towards the towers of Canary Wharf. For an instant he had a memory of watching a crane demolish a bombed-out building with a giant smashing ball, and caught a whiff of sparking blue flashes from the overhead wires of the trams on a damp but sunny day when his father had taken him to work with him in Poplar, in the East End of London.

When he walked into the pub it was already starting to fill up. He caught sight of Wetherton, who was standing at the bar. In front of him were two pints of a particular Belgian beer they both favoured. They had once attended an Interpol course together in Brussels, and had discovered a decent watering hole near the Atomium - a curious building that was a relic of one of those trade fairs that used to be so popular in the fifties and sixties. Wetherton welcomed him with an easy smile and pushed the second glass carefully over to him. Erasmus accepted it and they moved across to a corner of the room where they could sit and talk more privately. The general hubbub around them meant they could not easily be overheard – unless the place was bugged or one of them (or both) were wearing a wire. Hiding in plain sight, talking in a public space, listening intently to what is said and unsaid – all these were traits and habits developed over the years and enhanced by training. Interpol had been quite refreshing in its approach to policing - less rigid and more open to novel approaches. What worked was what was important. This had certainly suited the nonconformist in Inspector Erasmus, and D.S. Wetherton had followed suit.

Erasmus laid his cards on the table. Wetherton listened carefully and answered succinctly:

No, he did not know Evans, but knew of him.

Yes, he did know that Evans was investigating the fracking murders.

Yes, he was able to confirm that Scotland Yard had not been handed the case and yes, MI5 were running the show. His friends in the anti-terrorist squad were not pleased at being squeezed out by the spooks.

Yes, he would be happy to do a little discrete digging – in fact he had already dug up more information about the 'Marstons' and confirmed that Robert Marston had been on HM Payroll – services unspecified.

Wetherton was slightly taken aback when Inspector Erasmus then asked for his advice. Did he think his strategy viable and was he carrying it out in the best way possible?

"Look Inspector – Julian – you taught me most of what I know and certainly taught me how to recognise most of what I don't know. Far be it from me to tell you how best to run things. But, as you ask, perhaps you should give your team a greater role in the investigation – use the potential and additional eyes and ears you have there."

Erasmus took note. He realised that, despite what he intended, he had still not been entrusting his team as much as he should. He was beginning to see how this strategy could operate more effectively. He needed to trust his team implicitly. There was only one way to find out if this would work, and he was determined to try.

32. Teamwork

Siobhan Wright was pleased, but nervous, to find herself on a flight to Edinburgh. She had not been back for several years – not since she had finished college and left home. She did not speak to her father, her one remaining parent, and had no siblings. At the same time she was pleased that Inspector Erasmus had entrusted her with the responsibility of finding out everything she could about Harriet and her niece. An aged aunt was her only living relative – apart from her cousin Rollo – and she needed to know about the early years, her upbringing and her youthful ambitions. At the same time she would be retreading her own path; she needed to make sure she did not let this interfere with her professional duties. She tried to relax as the plane taxied for take-off but her mind kept flitting between her own story and the one she sought to discover. It wasn't until they were airborne and the plane had finished climbing that she began to settle.

Toby Butterdale was confident he could overcome his natural reticence. He just needed time to gather himself together. His confidence had been boosted when Inspector Erasmus had simply said 'thank you' for keeping him informed. He was beginning to learn how the Inspector liked to work and he felt he could learn from him. Now he had been asked to find out more about Robert Marston's travels over the last couple of years – but he must be discrete. They had been warned off this case and it had been handed to Evans' lot. Butterdale was tasked with being a silent shadow, a slight breeze in the heat of the sun, an unnoticed and obscure figure moving lightly across the background of a busy painting. Butterdale was skilled at being ordinary and unnoticed; it was his strength, a natural skill, and he was happy to make full use of it, if it meant he could do his job well.

Erasmus had set the wheels in motion and would continue his own private exploration of the past that would, eventually, lead him back again to the present. Meanwhile his team would embark on their own explorations alongside the tasks he had set them; how they might fare he did not know, but he certainly cared. He cared not merely for the sake of his own plan, but for their sakes as individuals. Although he recognised the risks more than they did, he also felt they were able to handle them. He would not have sent them out unprepared. In so doing he was deliberately hiding himself from another would-be designer of the story, another masterteller. He had a strategy and he was deploying his troops accordingly.

～

And now the story divides into separate streams that will later meet up again and feed into a much larger river. The metaphor seems appropriate, given the fluidity and the opaqueness of the current narrative. Its flow is unpredictable and chaotic, its swirling motion dissolves into repetition, and repetition of repetitions, and becomes fractal, as the text of the narrative accumulates its own repeating tropes, memes and motifs.

33. Edinburgh

In the morning she ordered a taxi, planning to be in Musselburgh for eleven o'clock. She was ready by nine o'clock and had an hour to wait before the cab was due. She decided to walk over to the Royal Mile.

She went down to Princes Street, and crossed over the tramlines. She made her way to the bottom of the Mound and looked up at the tenement blocks that towered like tall cliffs above the modern world. A short way up the snaking road that was the Mound she cut right up the steep stone steps that ascended to the Mile. She had managed this flight many times before and still, every time she counted them, the number seemed to grow. She stopped to catch her breath, and ease the tightening in her calf muscles, just outside *The Janglin Geordie*, and turned to look back across to the New Town. She heard the rattle of bottles and the thump of barrels as they prepared for the day ahead. She heard the voices of hacks still in conversation from the night before, and the laugh of night-workers slaking their thirst.

When she reached the Mile she was halted by the sound and appearance of a military marching band, proceeding up to the Castle. She felt the beat of the drums in her limbs and the pipes filled her lungs with sound - she almost took the King's Shilling there and then!

~

When the taxi dropped her off at the end of a row of small cottages, each attired in the same grey slate tiling and built of solid grey stone, she felt she knew immediately what to expect. But she was mistaken. Beyond the row of terraced cottages, end on to the road, was a short gravel pathway that led to another wee cottage. The sign on the gate said *'Rose Cottage'*.

What might have been a croft, had it been located in the Highlands or the Western Isles, was here covered with a pale pink pebbledash. Roses grew in abundance, rambling throughout the garden and smothering the porch in subtle whites and pinks, together with one or two vibrant deep reds. Siobhan felt it necessary to make this an exemption to her personal policy of deeming all things pink beyond the pale – she had even planned to start a campaign for the abolishment of pink cottages nationwide when Toby had said it was too important a matter to leave to politicians! She rang the doorbell and an East Asian lady came to the door.

"Please to enter," she said, stepping back and ushering her in, "Miss McPhairson see you now."

"Thank you Pabin. Do come in dearie!" called a voice from within.

Miss McPhairson sat in an upright armchair in a well-lit living room overlooking the front garden. She was not the wee dainty woman Siobhan had imagined – though she didn't realise she had formed such an image until she met her. It was merely old age - as the youngsters call it - that kept the formidable woman in need of a live-in carer; only that made you forget that it was women like her who had won the war. She was not squeamish; she was not flustered; she was not easily shocked. All this Siobhan discovered in the first few minutes of their interview.

"Now tell me dearie, why are you really here? What is it you really want to know?" asked Jeannie McPhairson.

Siobhan was flummoxed. The wind had been taken out of her sails and she knew there was no point in trying to maintain the pretence. She presented her credentials: her driving licence and her WPC's badge.

"Well, I've no way of telling one way or the other, I'm sure," said Jeannie, "But I'll give you the benefit of the doubt. Mind you, I'll be checking up on you after you leave, you can be certain of that."

Miss McPhairson was a woman of some distinction in her own right. It was she who had first introduced her god-daughter Harriet to the Oxford Recruiters. Harriet was a fine girl – headstrong, yes – but handsome, athletic and intelligent. She had a gift for languages and was quite at home with science and mathematics. She had to take some credit for that herself as she had often hosted Harriet during the holidays keeping her occupied with tasks domestic and educational. She had also taught her the rudiments of cryptography. Harriet had gone up to Oxford as expected – and had done very well – but she had rejected the Recruiters' advances and chose to steer her own course through life.

"What about her niece, Katrina?" asked Siobhan.

Jeannie McPhairson paused for moment – it seemed she paused for longer than should have been necessary just to gather her thoughts. But it was no momentary lapse, no senior moment – it was necessary. There was much to tell but it might need a degree of arranging. Or perhaps it was best to plunge straight in.

"Well, dearie, you see Katrina isn't really Harriet's niece, you know – she's her cousin. She was much younger, of course; she was related on her father's side of the family. She came into Harriet's care when just thirteen; her parents were killed in a plane crash – somewhere in Africa. Not that any of that's important. But you should know that the Recruiters took a shine to her too and she did respond to their advances. After University she spent a year in London and was then posted overseas. I have heard nothing of her since, I'm afraid."

Siobhan realised that Miss McPhairson knew nothing of recent events, as they pertained to Harriet and Katrina. She decided not to tell her about them. But Jeanie McPhairson was made of sterner stuff.

"I suppose they must be dead now, as you're here asking so many questions about them?"

Siobhan, held in Jeannie's gaze, looked straight back at her and nodded – yes, they were dead.

"Well I hope you get to the bottom of it – whatever it is. I don't need to know the details, I'm sure."

The interview was at an end – though it was unclear exactly who had been interviewing whom. Siobhan got up to go and as she did so Jeannie McPhairson rose slowly, went to the dresser, opened a draw and took out a small package which she handed to Siobhan.

"You can open it later, dearie. It may be useful to you."

After Siobhan had left Miss McPhairson, she went for a walk along the coast. The fresh sea air helped to clear her head. She knew she had more pieces to the puzzle but she had no idea how they might fit together. Her job, at the moment, was just to do as she was doing. Her data would be pooled when she returned to the office – perhaps it would have some significance then that she could not yet see. She tried not to ponder these questions too much and realised she had walked further than she had intended.

When she reached her hotel it was already late in the afternoon. The maid service had tidied the room as expected, though the TV was oddly positioned, as if someone might have been adjusting the wiring at the back. Perhaps the maid had been dusting – but the back of the set had certainly not been dusted. She decided not to use her mobile in her room, nor to use the room phone except to order a newspaper for the morning. Perhaps she was being overcautious – paranoid even – but she thought it best to be particularly careful.

She decided to change hotels, moving to the Scotsman Hotel on North Bridge. She seemed to have the natural reflexes of a professional – Evans had seen this in her even though she was, as yet, unaware of it herself.

She decided to use a pay phone – not that it was easy to find one – but when she did she simply called her own number at the office and left an agreed codeword. Inspector Erasmus would be able to pick it up and understand that she had completed her interviewing of Miss McPhairson. He would also understand, by virtue of the method of communication, that someone might be on to her.

Erasmus had warned her of the danger attendant upon her mission, but he had foreseen that something like this might happen. When he picked up the message he was angry – angry with himself. There was nothing he could do now except wait.

Siobhan hired a VW Golf automatic from a local firm at the airport. She submitted herself to the necessary 'paperwork', though it was all computerised in fact. She set off that same evening at about seven o'clock, just after rush hour, aiming to take advantage of less traffic on the roads overnight. She would avoid the motorways and take the switchback A68 down through the borders. She was familiar with this route, though she had not driven it for several years now, and had coffee and chocolate breaks planned at regular intervals en route.

It was almost seven in the morning when she arrived home exhausted. She left another message on the office answer phone then collapsed onto her bed. She slept till just after noon. Then she got up and had a shower. Forty-five minutes later she was on her way to the office.

34. Evans

Evans was quite mistaken to think that his easy intimidation of Toby Butterdale was sufficient. He hadn't bothered to keep a trace on him subsequently. He thought he was weak and would do as he was told. Nothing to worry about there.

WPC Wright was another matter entirely and he was curious to know how she would progress in her career. He would make sure they kept a close eye on her.

Toby was able to use Evans' neglect to his advantage, even if unwittingly so – it was the sort of good fortune that Toby attracted by dint of his apparent ordinariness and self-effacing nature. Erasmus had seen in him the advantage of this natural disposition and was not averse to making use of it. In time it would prove to be his salvation.

Toby began his investigations into Robert Marston by studying a photocopy of the pages from his passport. He confirmed these entries by cross-referencing with flight records, made available under anti-terrorist surveillance legislation. He made sure to make his enquiries seem as innocuous as possible, requesting general passenger details and focussing deliberately on aircrew and foreign travellers. However, he detected one possible discrepancy – anomaly rather. At first it had seemed to be a simple mistake, but he had looked at it again, more closely, had rechecked the dates and times carefully. No-one could possibly be in two places at once – unless they existed as quantum phenomena, and he was pretty sure that Marston did not – *most probably* did not – co-exist in the quantum dimension. He chuckled to himself, as if he might store that one up for a rainy day when he needed cheering up and there was no cricket to watch. He had noticed that Marston's itinerary was faulty, as a bowler's action might be faulty. He examined it more closely, and the likeness struck him.

The coincidence, the uncanny likeness. Had the photo-recognition systems at the airports been fooled? Was this Marston at Heathrow in September? Could it actually be a someone closer to home? He felt awkward about this line of enquiry but realised he needed to investigate his boss's movements around that time – if only to remove the anomaly. He began to research the Inspector's movements, he began to follow him, starting from a time about three years ago, a good eighteen months before he became his Sergeant. He found nothing – or nothing to link him to Marston in any way. Perhaps he was looking at this the wrong way round? Perhaps someone had been taking advantage of the similar looks - coincidental – between Marston and the Inspector. He wondered if the National Immigration database had been hacked and, if so, who would have been capable of doing it. What motive could they have had? He was raising more questions than answers but that was the nature of the business – "leave no stone unturned and always expect to find the unexpected" – that's what Inspector Erasmus had said – admittedly with a hint of ironic self-consciousness.

As he studied some of the tapes from the airport he noticed that Marston was sometimes greeted by a young woman. She was distinctive but always wore dark glasses and a headscarf so he could not get a facial recognition on the computer ID system. Still, it was something to note. But now his research must take him out of the office and away from computers. It was time for some old-fashioned police work. It was time to use his eyes and ears.

Marston had a registered business address in addition to his false home address. He would start there. The managed offices had a regular doorman. He saw that he habitually went for lunch at 12:30 every day, at the nearby Turkish café. He started to do the same. The doorman kept mostly to himself but spoke easily with the proprietor and his son. He liked to do the crossword whilst eating his lunch.

Toby was stuck on the crossword. He sat in his usual place, adjacent to where the doorman sat. He saw that Toby was stumped and offered to help him.

"Need 'elp with that bugger, eh? Name's John, John Redport"

He held out his hand and Toby accepted the gesture and shook it. "Well, if you don't mind. That's very kind."

The next day was not one of Toby's regular days and he resisted the temptation to appear at the café at lunchtime. The day after that he was back in place. When he saw John he asked if he could join him at his table. They compared notes on the crossword. Toby was certainly learning about cryptic clues and how to interpret them. His interest in words was typically more literal and his inclination more towards number puzzles, like Sudoku. Redport had been in his current job for nearly three years now and knew everyone who came and went. Toby let him talk freely, without probing for anything or anyone specific. Patience was his ploy. They compared notes on characters: Toby's office mates and their cliques; Redport's surveillance of all human kind as he cast his benevolent gaze upon them from the sanctity of his temple doorway. He bemoaned the newcomers: nice enough most of them, but foreign and without the knowledge and bearing of 'us old-timers'. Eventually he spoke about Marston:

"Always thought there was something strange about him. Couldn't say why at first but then I realised. He was a geologist of some kind, see? But he didn't know his sapphires from his amethysts. My wife's ring – we were gonna pawn it see, as we were in need of a few bob at the time. Asked him, I did. He was very nice about it and studied it carefully but he says it was sapphires and I know for a fact it weren't."

Toby also found out that Marston lived south of the river, near Hampton Court. He recalled without hesitation that Redport had once asked him to call him a taxi to take him home to *"41, Rolands Crescent"*. "Army training," he said, tapping the side of his temple with his right forefinger. Toby was suitably impressed.

Rolands Crescent was a pretty little row of terraced houses just off the main road. Small gardens, well kept, and cars parked on the opposite side of the road. Toby set about establishing his credentials in the locality and merged seamlessly into the background of everyday life around East Molesey.

35. Thermopylae

Jeannie McPhairson was nobody's fool. She knew – even if Siobhan didn't – that she was in danger. The reason that had brought that nice young girl to her door would be the same reason that brought others. She prepared.

Pabin was advised of the situation and knew exactly what to do. She was not only Miss McPhairson's carer, she was also her bodyguard. She had been one of the first female Gurkha soldiers recruited into the armed services and had seen action in both Iraq and Afghanistan. Herself the widow of a Gurkha soldier, she had been with Miss McPhairson now for more than ten years. She prepared the cottage's defences – old fashioned but effective – nothing too reliant on computers, apart from the CCTV units. She checked these were working and still well hidden – except for the dummy installations, which were designed to be found. She set the switches on the radio-controlled devices around the property. She notified Max at the Post Office, so he would be on the lookout for strangers. When all this was done she reported back to Miss McPhairson.

"Now it's just a question of biding our time and waiting. There's nothing else to be done." Miss McPhairson returned to the bridge problem she had been studying.

In the afternoon they played their usual game of whist. In the evening, after supper, they listened to the wireless. At a quarter to eleven they went to bed. The next morning Pabin cycled to the shop, as usual, for the daily provisions and some spare AA batteries.

Two days later the first signs were seen. Max reported that two men had been spotted down by the beach – apparently bird-watching. He suspected there was something not quite right because, although they seemed to have the appropriate equipment, they did not seem to have the appropriate knowledge. Jimmy Colston, a boy from the village, had asked if he could take a look with their binoculars. He'd spotted a bird that might have been a Curlew. When he pointed it out one of the men said it was just a Pheasant. Later in the day a motor cruiser arrived in Leith.

When they came, they were ready for them. They spotted the car up on the hill towards North Berwick. It came along the main road in the morning, not long after breakfast. This was an obvious approach, and in daylight, but these overconfident people were not worried about being seen. She had thought they might approach under cover of darkness, but these people were not worried about being seen; overconfident undoubtedly. Once they had completed their mission they would simply disappear. The thunder flashes would not perhaps be so useful after all. But they had planned their defence as offence and Jeannie was prepared to make the first move. It would be a battle of nerves against rigid certainty, of one fundamental belief against another – the time for cultural relativism was over. The line was drawn and such blatant intolerance could no longer be tolerated. She felt a sudden surge of pride and exhilaration. Pabin had taken up a sniper's position some two hundred yards to the north-west, hidden among the remains of an old shepherd's hut but with a clear line of sight to the cottage. From there she had an excellent view of the approaching enemy.

The car was halted by a single shot to the nearside front tire. They heard nothing to suggest it was other than a stone or a nail that had caused the puncture. Instead of stopping to change the wheel they proceeded on foot, in open view. As they got closer to the cottage they took cover. Pabin still had one in view and fired another shot. The man yelped and fell back, wounded in the thigh. The other man dashed towards the outhouse at the side of *Rose Cottage*. Her next shot somehow missed. Jeannie had seen what had happened and was prepared. The man came in through the back bedroom window. Before he could open the door to the front room he was dead. He had tripped a wire and set off a strategically placed grenade. Pabin immediately started to run back towards the cottage. Before she could reach the hedge at the bottom of the garden a shot rang out and she fell to ground. Another group of men were approaching from the direction of the sea. They must have arrived by boat and climbed up the cliff path. When Jeannie failed to get a response from

Pabin she sensed something was up. She had heard the shot and was preparing for the worst. If the first attack had been a distraction then it had certainly worked, but she wasn't finished just yet. She knew it was time, this one last time.

The four men approached cautiously – they were uncertain about the explosion they had heard coming from inside the cottage. They took out the CCTV but Jeannie McPhairson was still able to see them as they drew closer, thanks to the hidden cameras and the laptop that had been placed on the table in front of her. She poured some more tea from the flask on the table and sipped the sweet drink, taking pleasure from its lasting memories. Then she got up, slowly, and moved to the kitchen.

"The time has come, at last," she said to herself calmly.

~

The Fire Officer said that there had been a gas explosion. Completely destroyed the place. Five other bodies found, as well as the old lady's. Also noted that there was a vehicle along the road with a punctured tyre – no sign of the driver but there was a pair of binoculars and a bird identification book on the back seat. One other thing. There seemed to be fragments of what must have been an old wartime hand grenade – presumably kept as a souvenir.

Siobhan thanked him for this unofficial report. When she put the phone down she almost cried – but then she stood up and walked to the window, biting her lower lip in stoical defiance. "Good for you, Jeannie McPhairson!" she said to herself, "Good for you!" She heard nothing of Pabin and assumed she must have escaped or been sent away deliberately before the attackers arrived.

Siobhan guessed that the men had been after what Jeannie McPhairson had given her. While she could have felt guilty, she instead felt honoured; McPhairson had entrusted her with something important. Exactly what it was she held in her possession she did not yet know. It was still safely in the bottom of her bag, unopened. Erasmus had called a meeting for the next morning, over in Mournley, and they would find out then.

36. Reading

The doctors said that his concentration was likely to be affected at first. Erasmus was irritated by a lack of concentration, by an inability to shut out all, to inhabit another world. He struggled to finish the Shelley biography, while on a corner table other titles piled up - interesting dust jackets - but remained untouched. The doctors said the pills would kick in after a few weeks. He wondered if the price was worth paying. He persevered.

He knew that the distraction from reading – the real reason – was that he was already engrossed in another book. It was not a book that he was reading, it was a book in which he existed. It was not something that he could easily explain to others, even if he had wanted to; he could hardly explain it to himself. It was an ongoing process, a continuous exploration of time and place and being.

He made a conscious effort to move away from the intensity of production, to embrace the luxury of others' writing. He discarded the Shelley biography, temporarily. Sometimes he would engage with puzzles: crosswords, sudoku, bridge or chess problems; other times he would drift across the titles ranged on the shelf, remembering those he had read, noting those he would re-read, and lamenting those he knew he would never read again.

He understood, from his own experience, that a reader would browse and scan the contents, the arrangement of chapters, the author's biography – and then read sequentially until either he reached the end or grew bored and discarded the book. On one occasion he had himself deliberately chosen not to continue reading a novel that seemed to be deliberately toying with the Reader. He felt it was the only option open to him, as an intelligent Reader, by which he could exert his independence from the text and its omniscient narrator-*cum*-manipulator.

It was getting late in the day and he had work to do: reports to read and some exam papers to mark – examinations for Detective Sergeant. This was an entirely different sort of reading, one that required an attention to detail and a rigorous application of the given marking scheme. He knew that the marking would be normalised, to prevent a bias that was either too generous or too harsh, but he still wished to be as consistent as possible. This was his third year of marking exams and he wondered if that would be enough for him.

Swiftly his mind cleared of all else. He watched himself engaged in this activity from some hitherto undiscovered vantage point. He operated simultaneously in an absorbed manner as he assessed each paper and, at the same time he abstractly observed, and noticed that he was doing so.

Daylight had gone completely. He packed away the papers and completed the associated administrative records. He went into the back garden to view the stars. He traced a few familiar constellations and made a mental note to check this month's astronomical map in the Saturday paper. He went back indoors and tried to listen to a live concert by the London Philharmonic, from Smith Square, but his mind was still working overtime and, from somewhere previously unexposed in the light, a question rose to the surface – one which he knew he must try to answer.

Somewhere there was a book concerning imagination. It began with a general survey of contemporary psychological theories of creativity and ranged into the realms of metaphysical meditation. It discussed 'flow' and Zen Buddhism. He thought it might be useful for his purpose, to understand how things come into existence in the mind. Whilst looking for this particular volume he found another, that referenced the poet Coleridge. He latched onto the distinction between *Fancy* and *Imagination*, realising that even his own report writing exhibited both conscious organisational features and an unconscious arrangement of material. He also recognised its relevance to his own peculiar endeavour, to the creation of the book he had now begun to write. At last he felt tired enough to go to bed.

He read no more till the weekend, when he opened the newspaper to look for June's astronomical chart. He took note of where the major planets were and checked again where he might, with the aid of binoculars, discover the M31 Andromeda galaxy. This was virtually the extent of his reading – apart from official paperwork – over the last few days. However, he had by no means been idle. He had instead been writing extensively. This writing had, so far, been hidden from sight. He would now start to reveal it and allow it to do its work in directing, and misdirecting, his counterpart.

37. Writing

'Write about what you know about', as the adage says. Good advice. And Erasmus knew what he was writing about. What had been less sure, but was now becoming much clearer, was what else was being written and by whom.

The persistent distraction of his work, in addition to his hyper-aware state following Jennifer's death, caused his reading to grind to a halt. At the same time, Erasmus' writing, his self-creation, gathered pace and sped on as if nothing could stop it.

He knew he must let Toby and Siobhan discover their evidence. Each had a story to tell. As yet he did not know what that was and he looked forward to their reunion in the chapter he planned to write, provisionally called 'Gestalt'. He was not, as yet, in a position to control all that happened. He was still part of the flow.

There was still a Master-Writer, someone steering the narrative and exercising an overarching control. It mattered who it was but he was not yet ready to confront them and reveal them to others in the story. He had still to gather sufficient evidence, and to prepare himself for that moment. In the meantime he would write when able, as best he could, and continue to investigate the evidence as it was gathered and as it presented itself. There was time enough. He would be patient.

He began to keep a journal. It was not a diary – it did not record every day the mundane facts, like some inane Twitter account or indulgent and indiscrete blog. Instead it recorded as often as, and whenever, there was something of note to record: a thought or reflection, a realisation, an observation out of the ordinary, a moment in time. It was for no other to read; in fact he hardly reread it himself. It was a discipline, a Zen-like exercise in purgation. And alongside this exercise he began to write poetry. He adopted the disciplined form of the sonnet.

It was attractive to him inasmuch as it was succinct, composed, condensed, and conclusive. He liked its efficacy and its force. He had never engaged with poetry before but now began to understand the beauty of its density and the delight in consciously and unconsciously unpacking it.

But these were essentially external elements and experiences; Erasmus was 'writing' a story, his story, conducting his own investigation into things superficial and things hidden. His writing was an attempt to get behind the mask, to uncover the persona of another presence that he knew he could only get closer to by first moving in the opposite direction: Seek where it is not, that it may be found.

It was by writing explanations of this type that he was able to start to understand his own purpose and method. He began to liberate himself from the course of the narrative and to live among its structures and themes. He was here, now; he was in Scotland; he was at the table sitting opposite Evans at a meeting of heads of staff; he was in another place entirely that he could not yet see but knew existed. He was not only creating distance between himself and the other presence, he was also creating multiple tracks and paths, any one of which might be a dead-end or a trap. He began to feel the power of the enterprise he had undertaken, its ability to draw in all his energy and turn it into its own purpose. But he also knew he was as much controlled as controlling.

Journal (April 19th)

Been very busy researching the Family Tree online. Made a visit to Register Office in South London. Nothing exceptional. Distraction tactics proving effective so far.

Journal (April 24th)

I have sent WPC Wright to Edinburgh to interview Harriet's aunt. We need to know more of her background and that of her niece.

Butterdale is following up on Marston's travels over the last couple of years, looking for patterns and contacts that might explain and confirm some existing suspicions.

Journal (April 26th)

I must continue to provide a decoy to their activities and, at the same time, pursue my own line of enquiry.

Journal (April 29th)

No word from either Wright or Butterdale. Hopefully no news is good news.

Journal (May 4th)

Decided I must write chapters sequentially from now on. It's all coming together – beginning to gel.

38. Commentary

I had begun to realise that Erasmus was laying a number of different trails; I had to decide which to follow, and when. Should I stick with him on his road of rediscovery to see if he succeeded in creating his own independent existence? Should I try to track all the movements of his team members?

I had only limited resources and was in danger of spreading myself too thin. I needed to consider how best to tackle this diversification, which path or paths to explore. I decided to intervene with this commentary in order to re-establish my control over the story. Although I was in danger of distracting from the story – a criticism I have previously levelled at Melville – I felt I had no alternative. I had already admitted, implicitly at least, that Erasmus had an independent existence and that we were now engaged in a struggle that must end one way or the other. What the eventual outcome would be I had no way of knowing. I decided to put my plan into action without further ado.

~

Erasmus moved deftly from one place to another – a paragraph here in this chapter – another there in that chapter – and yet another paragraph in yet another chapter. He was building a sequential model non-sequentially, as if time itself were a jigsaw puzzle and the order in which he picked up and placed each piece was – if not arbitrary – then certainly not governed by strict rules of symmetry or chronology. He was, he hoped, disrupting the enforced narrative of someone, of another author.

39. Misdirection

Martin James Hogg was an actor, resting between roles. Today he was resting behind the counter of the local grocery store. Tomorrow and Saturday he would be resting at the local golf club, mowing and watering the greens and collecting lost balls to fill the buckets on the practice range. But on Monday he would not be resting, he would be acting - he had a job.

His agent had called him - after weeks of silence - and asked him to drop by as soon as possible. He had had something come in, something out of the ordinary and right up his street. He would say no more over the phone. Martin was curious and excited. He arrived in good time for his appointment and was almost immediately ushered into Robertson's office.

"Martin! Good to see you - do sit down. I almost said 'have a cigar' - only I haven't got any and you don't smoke, I think? Well, no matter. This is well paid and a really good prospect. If you carry this off you will be on a retainer - a 'nice little earner', though I say so myself. Top rate too - no skimping!"

Robertson was in fully-operational mode with no hint of the usual apologies or calls to thespian stoicism in the face of critical or financial adversity. He explained that someone was needed to play the role of an author, the writer of a thriller currently being written by person or persons unknown. Here's the 'script', if I can call it that. Read it carefully. You will be required to improvise your part - so there are no lines for you to learn as such. *Comprenez*? I see you do. Good. And there's no need for you to interview - you have the job solely on my recommendation."

"Oh and one more thing, my good fellow, you will be required to attend confession once a week - by way of a progress report to your employer. There's a schedule of different churches to attend. Verbal report only, an update at regular intervals - even if there's nothing to report, as such."

Martin nodded. No, he had no questions. All seemed straightforward enough – odd but straightforward. Yes, of course he was happy to undertake the role. They settled the where and the when and the payment schedule for the specific contract. All was in order.

Certainly this role was out of the ordinary but Martin needed the money. That he was, in some way, involved in a deception was clear. He assumed it was merely a harmless deception. Now he must work on his character, his motivation, and the backdrop against which he must extemporise.

Martin was philosophical. He realised that, as an actor, life brings greater and lesser roles. He was young enough to still have hope and yet old enough to be realistic when it came to accepting what was on offer. He knew of famous actors who had not been recognised until quite late in their careers, when some small part in a Hollywood blockbuster suddenly shot them to fame, and sometimes fortune too. He felt he was fortunate in that he was unmarried and had no-one but himself to support – oh and the cat as well, of course. But a fortune wouldn't go amiss! Later he would tell his girlfriend Dot, all about his new job. She would not understand or make any connection; she had insufficient self-awareness to do so. But she would be pleased for him, and pleased that he would be busy – too busy to bother her whenever he was at a loose end.

Later, when he was asked about the person he reported to, he could only say that it was a man he had spoken to but he had no idea what he might look like. His accent? Definitely RP, but with a hint of something – perhaps Surrey or Kent. At what turned out to be their final meeting he was given some typed instructions, which included an invitation to a Literary Festival where he would be acting as a competition judge. He wondered if it would be poetry, or plays, or short stories perhaps? He rather fancied the idea of himself as a judge. Of course he would only be acting, but he decided he would do so to the best of his ability, in order to justice not only to the role, but also to those who had submitted their work for judgement. He felt the burden of responsibility that good men must, and others sometimes do, and he responded accordingly.

I have heard it said that those who devote themselves wholeheartedly to some worthy project that is for the benefit of others are hiding something; I have heard it said that they are seeking to atone for some deed or omission in their earlier life. Perhaps that is so, I do not know. I am fairly confident, however, that Martin James Hogg was merely trying to do his best. Unfortunately, this tended to make him give too much and not keep enough back for himself. Hence he was prone to occasional bouts of depression and anxiety. But now that he had work to do, the sun was shining and the world was a good place for living. He felt refreshed and excited; he felt he had a purpose again.

40. The Meeting

Martin was nervous. They had arranged to meet for his first live session in the Globe Café. The very ambience of the location inspired his performance, he said afterwards. Whether that was so or not, his performance was certainly fit for purpose. It felt it was good enough to fool his counterpart – no mean feat in itself.

Erasmus approached the man sitting alone at the table. He seemed unprepossessing but he knew he must have a formidable imagination and was not going to underestimate him.

"Inspector Erasmus, I presume. Pleased to meet you. Do sit down."

He felt slightly disarmed by this welcome. He himself was no writer of fiction, had no notebooks, no sketches, no phrases gleaned from the incidental conversation of others. He had no profound insights to convey, no great conclusions to present, no metaphysical intuitions to divulge. He acknowledged the difficulty of the task ahead and deferred to his counterpart's greater experience in these matters.

"Tell me, Inspector Erasmus, how do you see it?"

"I'm afraid my view is merely partial – in both sense of the word. I agree that the matter is complicated and that we cannot simply attempt to tie up loose ends – that would be too obvious. Our Reader will certainly expect the unexpected."

"I agree, you are right. That being said, it falls to us to make something of all this. It is our responsibility and our duty."

They sat in the relative safety of a snug in the Bannockburn Arms, sipping a fine Glenmorangie and considering everything that had just been said – their calm conversation and the comparing of notes. They were approaching a handover point and Erasmus was not sure he was yet ready for that.

"I have no doubt you're ready for this Julian. No doubt at all. You have managed matters far better than anyone could have reasonably expected."

Erasmus recalled their conversation at a later date, after everything in this story had long since concluded, saying:

"I was flattered but slightly nervous too. Would I be able to take this responsibility and do justice to the story? Would I be able to complete my investigation successfully? I could only do my best. I felt that I was succeeding across several fronts. I had even introduced a completely new development in the story and this was about to reach a dramatic climax. As counterparts we knew each other's moves, each other's quirks and foibles, as if they were our own which, in a sense, they were. It did not matter, as I later found out, that this was only the author's mouthpiece."

But for now they needed to combine their efforts. Matters were moving to an ending and it needed to be good, it needed to be convincing. Neither one of them were as confident as they felt they should be, and neither one was as prepared as he would like to have been. But so it was. They agreed to join forces, to unite, and to struggle against the arbitrary referential forces of language and the totalitarian ideology of fanaticism alike. It was a curious alliance.

The next day Martin Hogg attended confession. He reported the conversation with Erasmus carefully, providing every detail. He confessed that he had lied.

41. Gestalt

Erasmus and his small team were assembled in an anteroom of the village hall in Mournley. Built in the mid to late nineteenth century, and refurbished recently with a grant from the European Regional Development Fund, this village hall was like many others: a stage hidden behind heavy faded drapes, large brown teapots used to pour gallons of stewed tea, old jumble sales items stored under the stage, together with trestle tables for cake stalls and the like, and a blend of human effort and worth that transcended any single generation. The modernisation, necessitated by a leaking roof, was generally sympathetic. They had kept the old floorboards - polished by years of small boys sliding across them with boisterous glee, but years of dust and dead insects, disturbed from high window shelves by ruffled curtains and high throws in timeless games of dodgeball, were gone - removed in the renovation.

Now the team were gathered together again, around a small table. Erasmus looked younger and fresher. Toby sat upright, exuding confidence, a confidence that only comes with a certain degree of self-knowledge; Siobhan felt proud to be there working among equals, all dedicated to the same cause; she was eager to share with them what she had discovered. They brought the pieces of puzzle they had each collected and tipped them out onto the table in front of them, literally or metaphorically.

Toby was first to go:

Marston - no geologist. Girlfriend - much younger than him, unidentified. Residence - Hampton Court. A safe house of some sort, probably MI5 or the like. Itinerary included Pakistan, Afghanistan and Liberia - other journeys abroad not documented in passport. Speculation: Role as blood diamond courier or similar possible.

Siobhan was next:

Harriet's cousin – Katrina. Harriet declined Oxford invitation to join MI5. Katerina successfully recruited. Last official posting to New York. May have gone underground to infiltrate eco-activist cells. No knowledge of her controller.

Jeannie McPhairson. Former SOE operative. Harriet Gordon's God-Mother. Knew more than she told but – after interviewing her – all hell broke loose. Evidence of criminal (possibly foreign) involvement in attack. Bodyguard now missing.

"And there's something else," said Siobhan, dipping into her bag and rummaging around. Finally she pulled a small package from the depths of her handbag and placed it on the table.

"What's this then?" asked Toby eagerly.

"I don't know, but Miss McPhairson said it may prove useful. I haven't opened it yet. I was waiting till I got back."

"Quite right," said Erasmus, "but before we do let me add my tuppence worth to the pot, just to keep it boiling.

Erasmus could not easily include them in the more abstruse reasoning of his enquiry, in pursuit of the Author, but he was able to tell them something of his own researches and to pull together the seemingly separate strands they had gathered between them.

"From what we've got so far I think we can reasonably suppose that Marston was Katrina's controller – at first. Later they became lovers. After that? – I don't know"

"Do you think she had anything to do with his murder?" asked Toby.

"Yes, I do, but I don't think she murdered him herself – merely allowed it to happen, perhaps even arranged it."

"Why do you think that?" asked Siobhan.

"She didn't have to do it herself. Look, we have evidence of her manipulation of people and circumstances – look at her role at the protest camp. She was also, I believe, likely to have been involved in some way with Sam Grainger's death – though I have no conclusive proof. What I can say is that he was used by her as a courier – for drugs at least. Last week's drugs squad raid confirmed that. Got him on surveillance video.

133

He was clean, remember? It wasn't for his own personal use. And he may have been courier for more than just drugs; forensics are still piecing together the bomb fragments from the fracking site here in Mournley. If that is the case – and even if he wasn't the mule – someone got hold of the explosives from somewhere. The interesting question is: from whom? And why was it necessary to kill Marston?"

He turned to Siobhan and indicated the package on the table. Carefully she undid the neat knot in the string and unwound it from the brown paper that it held together tightly. The paper itself was crisply folded with symmetrical pleats and tucks. She slowly opened it up to reveal a small inlaid wooden box . Erasmus took note: it was made of an African hardwood and was decorated with fine carving. He admired the quality of the craftsmanship. The box contained a ring and a letter. The letter appeared to be in code and the ring was, judging by its weight, more than merely nine carat gold. It clasped a deep blue diamond. There was also a colour photograph of Katrina as a young child, sitting next to her mother and holding hands with a man who was presumably her father. He was dressed in a dark suit and paisley tie. He was tall and elegant and handsome. He looked as if he might be from the highlands of East Africa. On his right forefinger was the same ring that they now had in their possession.

"Why would anybody have wanted this ring so badly that they'd be prepared to kill for it?" Siobhan asked.

"I think I know why," replied Erasmus, "I think this is evidence of a compromising nature. Katerina's father was an apostate in the eyes of his own family and disowned by them – having chosen to marry outside his Faith. I learnt this in my research over the last few weeks."

Siobhan looked somewhat surprised. She had not realised that the Inspector had also been making his own independent enquiries.

"I'm sorry I didn't tell you before," he said, "but I needed to have the facts corroborated independently – which you have succeeded in doing. My thesis is that some time later, exactly how is unclear, Katerina's father came into a large sum of money. It remains unclear precisely where this originated but it is possible that her grandfather had once been

Chancellor to the Emperor. Now there are others who need to finance their expansionist aims and access to the information contained in this letter – which I believe is not in code but actually a set of account numbers - will allow them to obtain millions of dollars to fund their ambitions. How they came to hear of its existence – whether through luck or, more likely, torture – we may never know."

"Jeannie McPhairson must have known that I would inevitably lead them to her. I'm afraid my actions acted as a catalyst for that terrible day!" cried Siobhan.

"That may be, but they would have found her sooner or later. You can't blame yourself. Once they knew that Harriet didn't have what they wanted, they were bound to search further afield," replied Erasmus.

"Well, this is turning out to be a bit like a cursed-treasure hunt," said Toby. "Shouldn't we share this evidence?"

"What evidence? With whom? After all we're off the case, are we not? Erasmus continued: "It's all very circumstantial. I supect the *powers-that-be* are even now busy disseminating some highly unlikely but necessary cover story for the events we've described and undoubtedly occurred."

The efforts of the team had proved successful and Erasmus had learnt a lot about both his team and himself. But the next move must be his own, alone.

42. On the Security and Intelligence Agencies

A government spokesman has stated: *"We are committed to increasing the number of women in the security and intelligence agencies, particularly at a senior level,"* and again: *"We are committed to ensuring the most talented people succeed and reach top positions, regardless of gender, ethnicity, sexuality or disability."*

Curious. Curious that the apparent inconsistency passes without comment; that the implicit contradiction is unacknowledged; that the opportunity remains available.

So, what of statistics? There are more women in the population than men: slightly more are born or survive infancy, and many more survive to a greater age. Nowadays there are far more women in the workforce, continuing a trend begun during the Industrial Revolution and reinforced during the two World Wars. Therefore, if we have similar numbers of males and females in the workforce, should we not expect:

1   more women in the security and intelligence services?

2   more women at a senior level in these services?

If all else were equal and no other variables were involved, then the answer would be yes. But all else isn't equal and there are other variables involved.

We are seeking the *"most talented"* – regardless of ... etc ...

So now we need to define "talented" and also, I suggest, "willing and able". Candidates may be talented (definition awaited) and have the ability – all else being equal – to perform the job.

I might regard myself as talented and having the ability; others might even agree with my (albeit immodest) self-assessment. But I may not be *able or willing* to do the job. Why not? Here are several possible reasons:

1 I am not inclined to do the job.
2 I do not like the culture of the workplace.
3 I have ethical objections to the sort of work that is carried out by these services.
4 I have other interests I prefer to pursue.
5 I have other responsibilities I must fulfil e.g. looking after children or an elderly relative (perhaps an aged parent, who suffers from longevity).
6 I do not possess the necessary temperament required for the sort of work that must be done.
7 I haven't been asked.

Once these factors are taken into account we may not have a simple statistical target to aim at or expect, instead we may have distortions due to other societal influences. Who in a family typically nurses the young and the elderly? Who is typically excluded from these duties? On the other hand, such differences might cancel out each other.

But let us continue further along this path of reasoning. If such factors were spread evenly among the population then we might expect *more* women in these agencies than men and *more* women in senior positions than men. And once we have reached that place, then would we not say that the most talented have succeeded?

Well *no*, actually. Why not? Because like Justice, talent is blind. It is perfectly possible that our security and intelligence services be staffed entirely by women.

Personally I look forward to that day when I shall be free to play golf or paint or carve perfect lines in the well groomed grass whilst seated on my motorised lawnmower, and not have to trundle off to work every day, returning home much later to a signed copy of the Official Secrets Act. And 'mum's the word'.

43. MI5

Since the loss of Sir Lionel Wilberforce, much had changed behind the crumbling walls of Britain's Secret Services. Not only had there been changes among staff at all levels, but there had also been a general election. Such an event was always a cause of some disquiet, this time no less than usual. Although a majority government had been returned, this did not, of itself, mean that there were fewer tremors. In fact the ideological predilections of the new government, freed from the shackles of its previous coalition constraints, was even more radical and sure of itself than ever. And it was in power.

Evans had been summoned by Sir Reginald Snow to a meeting of heads of staff. 'Reggie' was a safe pair of hands – a man for the time being - and generally thought not to be too imaginative. However, he was adept at doing what was required, or at least he appeared to be. Not that he was not adept but rather he had an ability to move in more than one direction simultaneously, concealing his hand like the true poker player he was. He had served his time in Berlin - was stationed there when the Wall came down - and was past normal retirement age, but he was needed now. So it was that Evans found himself summoned to HQ for a post-COBRA meeting. The fragmentation that occurred after Libya and Syria, combined with the prominence of ISAL in Iraq, had become a terrorist threat that undermined the security of the nation and the safety of its citizens. Hearts and minds were being lost because of weak and woolly liberal thinking, on the one hand, and complete totalitarian control on the other – two normally opposed forces unwittingly united in the advancement of a common cause.

It was clear that the democratic defences had been breached and that the terrorists had the upper hand. Their methods, arbitrary and sporadic, spontaneous, and uncertain, rendered them virtually undetectable. Social media truly had become anti-social. It had become politicised as a weapon of fanatical anarchy, of absolute rule and dogma, of instant justification and demonic release. The summoning was a clear indication that there was – at last – an appetite for resistance, a desire to take the fight to the enemy, and a sense that all was about to change. Evans only understood this in part, but some of his colleagues were already ahead of him in their appreciation of the situation. This was not mere office politics, this was a reality shift that would alter the course of human history. He would have considered such a claim melodramatic but, from a pragmatic perspective, he agreed something definitely needed to be done.

Reggie called the meeting to order – or rather, he cleared his throat – in his unique and unassuming way, and the various conversations around the room fell silent.

"Thank you gentlemen, and ladies," he said, courteously acknowledging their presence. None took offence at his old world chivalry – he was too cuddly to be considered chauvinist. Carolyn Dubree, head of IT and Comms, was in fact a secret admirer – she wanted to take him home and look after him. Reggie was the sort of chap who seemed like a helpless child on the first day of term at a new school. All the bullies seemed to gravitate towards him as if he were inviting them to see how hard they could punch him. But she knew his vulnerable appearance and gentle manner belied a sharp mind and an astute awareness of others' motives and what it was that made each of them tick.

"Thank you for coming today at such short notice. You will be aware that COBRA has just met. We have our orders. It is our job to enact the policies and decisions that have been agreed by our elected political masters. But we shall do so not only with customary diligence and determination, but also with a skill and deftness that will draw upon all our collective experience. It will demand a willingness to embrace change and to adapt more rapidly than ever before. We will need to improvise in ways that we have not had to do since the old days of the Berlin Circus."

Reggie's speech became more sonorously intoned, more Churchillian by the minute with every chosen word – he was in his element, inspiring the troops! His fine oratory was greeted by polite and generous applause, some of it genuine. Whatever you thought of him, Reggie knew his stuff. Perhaps his 'safe pair of hands' was more than that; perhaps this was his final fling, the chance he had been waiting for all these years – the chance to make his mark.

The meeting was not long and protracted; it was succinct and to the point. But it was radical in its outcome. Each section was to operate as an independent unit with only a small degree of central control. Resources were to be reallocated accordingly. This fashion had been seen before by those who had been around long enough to see that the wheel turns full circle. But that was not all. There was to be an accelerated recruitment drive at every level – the best people for the job regardless of background and experience. Reggie explained that this was required in order to get up to speed with the nature of the new radical terrorist threat. But it was also necessary at another level. As Sir Lionel, his predecessor, had realised, the whole story was in danger of revealing too much, of effecting extreme subversion, of jeopardising MI5's operational capability, of creating its own terror. And he couldn't allow that to happen.

After the meeting, Reggie took Evans aside.

"Look Ted, I know you're already looking after the business about Marston, and I certainly don't wish to interfere. But - and there is of course always a *but* - I think *you* may be in the best position to strengthen the squad, as it were."

"How so?" asked Evans.

"Well it's this Erasmus chap. We think he could be useful – well vital, actually – to our bringing things under control. Not just with Marston but with the whole business."

"I see," said Evans (though he was sure he didn't – at least, not yet).

"I fear we may already be too late and, if so, then our only real hope resides in someone who is more aware of and closer to the heart of the matter than we are. Our agent is still out there but she is no longer our agent, and I don't think she's theirs either – she's gone rogue on us, old boy! We do not have access to the sort of information we need.

But Erasmus does – or will have soon. He's our man. And we must get to him before she does."

Ted Evans was not sure whether he should phone the men in white coats or just go along with him for the time being; the whole scheme sounded preposterous! He took a deep breath, held his own counsel, and thanked Reggie for his trust in him. He would be on the case straight away. He had been keeping tabs on Erasmus, and his team, and knew where to find him.

This was only partially true: he had mislaid Butterdale; lost WPC Wright somewhere in the Highlands, or so he understood – incorrectly as it happened – and only knew that Erasmus was presently revisiting the haunts of his earlier life. Later he would discover that Erasmus had flitted off to Spain, at a moment's notice, and for no apparent reason.

Reggie had also kept his own counsel. He knew what had happened in Musselburgh. He knew that Harriet and Katerina were somehow involved. And he knew that Katerina, having gone underground in order to infiltrate terrorist cells, was now out of control. Lionel's brave but foolhardy action had not brought about any resolution to the matter; it had merely satisfied his own honour and vanity. Of course, what Reggie did not know, was that Sir Lionel had intended to dispose of their renegade himself. He was unfortunate in that he happened to stumble across a party of Al Shabad militants, engaging in a deadly firefight with them.

Evans was not privy to this information but he knew enough about Marston's 'pupil' to understand that something had gone seriously wrong. No one had seen this coming: not the Psychs up at Darringford; not the Gryphons down in Mumbury – who re-evaluated core skills on a routine basis – nobody had noticed anything out of the ordinary. Nobody had predicted this.

Evans had always had his doubts about the value of Psychs – those people who tried to probe into the minds of others to identify what makes someone suitable for this sort of work. This only confirmed his opinion. This was clear evidence. But all this was by the by. He needed to reach Erasmus. To do that he first needed to find him – and to find him before she did.

141

~

It was certainly useful to have MI5 involved. Their ability to take a privileged overview was akin to his own and it provided an opportunity to obscure, as much as reveal, critical elements of the plot. Although MI5 possessed an awareness of other characters in the story, they seemed unconcerned about the relativity of their own position. Perhaps this was because they had already realised the arbitrary nature of existence. In some way their existence was not entirely of his making and even he did not know precisely what they were up to behind the scenes.

44. Spain

Erasmus had not been to Spain since the failed post-Franco coup . At that time he had been visiting Barcelona as a student; now he was going back, but not to Catalonia – instead he was going to Andalusia, in the far south. He wanted to visit the *Alhambra* in Granada. He was continuing to lay a series of related and unrelated trails. It was early summer and very pleasant there, but not yet too hot to move about freely in the full sun.

He had been planning this trip, he realised, for a long time. The idea had been brewing for perhaps a decade or more without ever surfacing and becoming a reality. That was no longer the case. He had begun to resurrect his knowledge, revisiting his phrase book, and studying the maps and transport options available over the internet.

He was surprised at how readily the language returned to him. He had only a smattering of phrases still to hand when he embarked but he soon rediscovered more in the nooks and crannies of his mind. And his brain uncluttered, and he began to think, without thinking directly, in the Castellano of his youth.

He was lodged in the narrow streets of the old city in Granada. The taxi had dropped him off nearby but he had had to search for the tiny square located in the midst of ancient cobbled alleyways. This evening he would explore the tapas bars; tomorrow he would visit the Alhambra.

∼

Evans arrived later that evening, taking a taxi to a modern hotel on the other side of town. He was travelling light but his mission weighed heavily on his mind. The turnaround in strategy at MI5 had certainly caught him by surprise. He was tasked with making the approach and had licence to reveal as much as he needed to, in order to persuade his contact. He did not know what reception he would get. He would need to check the lie of the land – no hasty moves. He had already made the mistake of underestimating Erasmus' Detective Sergeant – he would not make the mistake of underestimating Erasmus himself.

Granada is a bustling little town – friendly to tourists and ready to entertain. Flamenco music and dancing takes place in the square every evening as you drink your *cerveza* or sip at *sangria*. This busking is intended to entice you along to one of the regular evening shows. And if you have seen the show already you can choose simply to move among the crowd and enjoy being a tourist. You can walk in the gardens and listen to the other tourists chatting without feeling that you are intruding or are unwelcome. It is fortunate that the economy in this part of Spain remains relatively healthy. Its main attraction is, of course, the Alhambra and the beautiful palace gardens of the Generalife. The Moorish design of the buildings and gardens, with their flowing waters and cool pools, is transcendent. Visitors can take the bus up the hill but it is far more satisfying to arrive on foot, with the satisfaction of reaching the goal by one's own effort, as if it were a pilgrimage. All this assumes you have managed to, or will succeed in, purchasing a ticket for your timed visit. All this Erasmus was to discover over the next few days.

Evans was biding his time, looking for the right moment to approach. He knew Erasmus by sight; they had met once before under rather different circumstances. This meeting would be unexpected and he did not know how Erasmus would react – either to their meeting or to the proposal he was authorised to convey.

Erasmus was enjoying himself. He felt that he might just have shaken off his counterpart, the Author. He felt relaxed enough to do some shopping – in Spanish. He had with him a pair of leather-soled brogues and these were too slippery on the local cobblestones. He went in search of a pair of open sandals – *'Jesus Boots'*, as they used to call them, in his neck of the woods, way back when.

As he wandered through the gardens Erasmus was aware that he was not alone. It did not feel like the presence of the Author. It was more as if someone had noticed him and had picked him out from amongst the other tourists. He did not think He was being followed but he did suspect that his movements were being watched. Whoever was doing it was highly skilled as he could not see who it was who might be watching him. Perhaps it was just a result of spending too much time in his own company, talking to himself.

Evans was skilled. He had been well trained and had many years of operational experience. He was a professional. He would be able to choose his moment. He suspected that Erasmus might be aware of his presence but he was confident he had not been spotted. That was good. Timing was all, especially in this line of business.

～

There was an exhibition in the Generalife museum. It was of a renowned flamenco guitarist and *chanteur*. Erasmus came across it quite unexpectedly and, to his delight, it was fascinating. The young lady on front of house duty was very knowledgeable and enthusiastic, without being at all over-bearing, and he felt a welcome guest in this haven, one that paid homage to a musician previously unknown to him.

Slowly Erasmus is starting to realise that each of the characters in this story is assuming a life of their own, just as he has done. He has no control over this. Even the Author would admit he no longer plans or prepares what is happening. It is happening. The story will reach its own destination in due course. He recognises the limits of his influence and relaxes into the moment, here in the museum, in the Generalife, in the Alhambra, in Granada, in post-Franco Spain.

Evans is completely unaware of Erasmus' state of blissful enlightenment; he is going about his regular business, that of spymaster and practitioner, in a typically prosaic fashion. He is, once more back in the field, only this time in highly unusual circumstances, unique in his experience. He hopes Reggie is right and knows what he's up to. Damn it if he doesn't!

It is time. He must make contact. There is no obvious way. He decides to make it easy for Erasmus. He sits at a table in the square mid-morning, and orders Turkish coffee and a glass of cold water. The waiter brings a local delicacy that is similar to fudge. It is sweet and and sickly, like the mixtures of the Middle East. Evans asks for a backgammon board, though he sits alone and there is no one else to play. Nearby there are a few other people seated at tables for coffee: an elderly couple enjoying these days of sunshine, a young mother and her baby, a young woman in dark glasses with a turquoise headscarf, tapping at her mobile phone.

It may be nothing; it may be something. Is this the girl who met "Witherspoon" in Highgate Cemetery? That seems to be the suggestion. But why should attention be drawn to it? Is there something key to understanding the plot? Is it merely a coincidence? Or is it, perhaps, just a young woman in dark glasses?

Evans watches as Erasmus approaches from the far end of the square in the direction of the old town. He has noted that Erasmus prefers to take his morning coffee in the shade and has seated himself at a suitable vantage point. As Erasmus approaches he looks up from under the sun shade over his table and catches his eye. Erasmus shows no surprise and walks over to Evans. He takes hold of the back of the chair in front of him and asks:

"May I?"

"Of course. Do sit down. Can I get you something to drink?"

"An Americano, please."

They sit in silence for a moment then engage in small talk – the weather, the tapas, the ticketing arrangements for the Alhambra – until the coffee arrives, and more sweet delicacies.

Erasmus studies the backgammon board, as if to consider his next move, though they are playing a different game.

"So, to what do I owe this pleasure?" Erasmus asks.

"Orders. Orders from above. Not *Him*, of course," Evans replies, pointing skyward.

"Yes, I see," Erasmus responds, smiling politely, "Why now? Why me?"

"Fair questions. Let me see if I can answer them."

And so saying Evans begins to lay out the background to, and purpose of, his mission here in post-Franco Spain, at this point in time, and in this particular place.

Ted Evans was, on this occasion out of his depth, and knew he was, but he was less willing to admit it. Erasmus realised this and made allowances for his professional pride, even if it were mistaken. He understood that Evans was simply doing his job and, after all, they were on the same side.

Evans explains Reggie's request – they need his assistance, his expertise, his degree of authorial awareness. He avoids mentioning anything about rogue agents, or Marston, keeping to the standard line on terrorism. He does not know that Erasmus is already way ahead of him on that subject. And he suspects that the closer he gets to the truth, the more in danger he will become. He has already seen what her friends are capable of.

"I see," said Erasmus. "So I am needed. Then I need to know everything that you already know and I do not."

"Agreed," replied Evans.

"And my team?"

"Not a problem."

"When do I start?"

"You already have."

45. Interruption

"Well, it seems as if Erasmus is being accepted into the fold – he is needed. I wonder if he expected this? I certainly didn't.

I had not thought that the story would take this direction. I had assumed I would know what was happening and what would happen – I was wrong. Erasmus has completely altered the direction of the narrative and has caused things to shift dramatically. He is a danger to me, beyond my control.

Perhaps I have created – or perhaps we, you and I, have created – a type of monster? Something inevitable, something beyond the normal limits of literary invention. He has presence, he has shape, he has history, he has existence. I begin to doubt my own abilities to manage the story. But I must try."

46. Pursuit

It was time. Erasmus had laid a series of trails, false trails, and dead-ends. He had disappeared into his own esoteric researches, surfacing only occasionally to continue his investigations. His counterpart, the Author – in overall charge of the narrative – was considerably weakened by his loss of control. Erasmus was preparing to turn, to reappear, and to confront. It was an existential challenge that he must face head-on.

～

Erasmus knew that he only had one chance to succeed. The element of surprise was on his side. Although he was not writing this story he was, to a significant extent, directing it by his own actions. Neither the Author nor the Terrorist could avoid his relentless pursuit. They would, eventually, realise that they must stand and wait. They could not run forever, nor could they mask their appearance without confirming it to him. The attempt to dissuade, to dissemble, to camouflage, was ineffective. By his pursuit of his own past, and the creation of his own existence, Erasmus had become their nemesis. But even he could be thwarted; even he might not control final events, as he would eventually discover.

～

Reggie was very hospitable. He had given Erasmus everything he needed: an office, a phone, a desk, a chair, a laptop, a codename, and a swipe-card to get in and out of the building. All this was quite in keeping with his new position – affiliated as he now was to MI5. However, Erasmus felt he was in danger of merely becoming entrapped in the conventions of the standard spy genre. That really was *not* him.

And so he set about pursuing his target: not the murderer of Robert Marston, or perhaps Sam Grainger, but the mind that guided the story in which he found himself, in which we all find ourselves – Reader and Writer alike.

He had turned the tables. Initially his counterpart had hidden himself and then pretended to reveal himself. When Erasmus first realised he was being observed and directed, when he took up the challenge bequeathed to him by his late wife, he began to make himself disappear into the story, deliberately. He had almost completed his carefully planned and executed manoeuvre. He knew how to find him, and where – it was only a question of when. It must be an oblique approach, nothing too obvious – that would give the game away. His counterpart must suspect nothing untoward. Even though he was aware of Erasmus' direction he could not yet see exactly where he was heading. He was as much in the dark as the rest of us; he was vulnerable.

~

Let us call him John, this counterpart, this originating Author, this fiction of narrative. He is writing this – or someone like him is. He is seated at a table by a swimming pool somewhere in Switzerland. He is watching the sea eagles fishing in the lake.

Reggie does not know who he is. No one does. Reggie only knows of his existence. His identity remains unknown, though that he exists, is certain. And now Erasmus is searching for him, he has gone into hiding somewhere in plain sight, the most difficult place to find anything or anyone. But that is not all. Erasmus is hunting for a killer too and, unknown to him or anyone else (anyone?) they are sitting not a stone's throw from each other. But that is not now and it comes later in the story.

~

John is waiting. He is waiting for Erasmus to show. He has stopped trying to follow him and keep up with him; he has let him go. Now he is watching and waiting.

He remembers waiting, many years ago, for his mother. He was standing in the park, next to the swings, watching the other children playing. He wasn't allowed to go on the swings; they were too dangerous. He had a bag of crusts to feed the ducks with. He was hungry and he ate some. He found a stick and used it to stir the water in the pond, looking for frogs and newts, that the ducks might have missed, hiding under the lily-pads. She was gone for a long, long time. At last she returned and they went to get ice creams. He thinks he has still not forgiven her – why else should he remember that day? But he knows he is able to wait – there's no need to rush. He has all the time in the world.

~

Reggie is anxious. He is becoming more agitated by the hour. His resources are stretched, his successes are overshadowed by his failures, and the P.M. wants blood. Even the Home Secretary, usually a firm ally, seems to have lost patience. He knows his strategy is working, but it needs time, and time is a scarce commodity right now. Where is Erasmus? What is he doing? Why hasn't he heard back from him?

He calls Ted Evans. Within the hour Evans is there. No, he has no news from Erasmus, Yes, he will find him. Yes, he is leading the search for al Kadassa. No, he won't forget to call in as soon as he has some news.

Reggie continues his fretting, pacing to and fro across the full width of his expansive office, from one view of the River to the other. Unlike his predecessor, Reggie is no man of action, as such. But he needs to do something to occupy his mind in a useful and productive way. He knows his strengths are in getting others to work well together and in overseeing organisational changes. Perhaps he should work to his strengths. He calls his P.A. and asks for the GCHQ duty liaison officer.

After a few minutes he receives a call back. Would it be ok if he dropped in later that day – flying visit – nothing formal – just a quick chat with Q Listening Section? Twenty minutes later, an unmarked car drove swiftly out of London and along the A40 before picking up the M40 en route to Cheltenham.

He must act. He casually enquires at Security if Mr Austin is available. "No, no he's not expecting me. If you could just say it's Reggie, Reggie Snow". He liked to maintain his old contacts informally, never introducing himself as Sir Reggie – that would be bad form.

Austin understands. He will place the commission. He understands it is *ex officio*, like the work in Berlin before. Yes, the channels are still open. Untraceable. *Mum's* the word.

~

It is growing lighter. Erasmus is moving into position; he senses the moment is coming. There is a nervousness in the narrative, a switching back and forth among themes, between paragraphs. As John would recall, sometime later, in conversation with Erasmus:

"You had decided it was finally time to make your move. Our meeting could be put off no longer. I had lost sight of you. I no longer knew what your next move was going to be. That is when I set up my replica for you to meet – I thought he did very well but, in the end, not well enough. Earlier I had watched from a distance as you struggled to make sense of the story – its development, its characters, and its plot – but now I knew you had taken control of things and you had not been fooled by my misdirection. You had the information that Katrina desperately wanted – the security box account numbers – and she had realised you must have them. I must have let that slip. Sorry, that was careless of me."

Of course Erasmus had already reasoned that she would be looking for him. Each was hunting and each was being hunted. The trap was closing in.

47. Terrorist

It is dark. He is asleep. Carefully she slides out from under the duvet, slips on a bathrobe and picks up her bag. She turns on the bathroom light and he mumbles in his sleep and turns over. When she has finished she steps out and takes the service staircase down to the ground floor. On reaching the exit by the rubbish bins she quickly dresses and leaves. He, of course, will never leave.

~

A girl, about sixteen years of age, is waiting for the delivery of a small package. She is waiting in the shade of an alcove near the village water pump. She is wearing a light-blue headscarf and grips the wrap in her bright white teeth, made brighter by the contrast with her black *hijab*. A jeep draws up beside her and a man hands her a holdall. She takes it without hesitation and retreats into the shadows, following the alleyways through the ancient souk and out into the suburbs.

When she reaches her destination, a small upstairs single room apartment, she swiftly disrobes and straps the bandoleer across her chest. She then quickly dresses again and kneels to pray. It is time. She must save the lives of her younger brothers. She must do as she is commanded. Finishing her prayers she leaves the small room where she has dressed and exits, heading straight to the market. She knows where the soldiers will be. She may even recognise some of them, young as they are, though she feels nothing.

An explosion rips through the market place, injuring, maiming and killing dozens.

Minutes before a mother called her small children to her and gave them a wicker basket and some money. She sent them to market to buy fresh fruit and bread for their mid-day meal. They stopped to stare at the soldiers by the Old Gate at the entrance to the market. The little boy sees his big sister on the other side of the street and starts to run over towards her . . .

~

She is deep undercover now. She is an eco-warrior - but only in name. Her purpose is otherwise. She is not interested in chalk downlands, or HS2, or fracking. She is only interested in making connections. She is only interested in making contact. She is finding common ground with her quarry, who she makes her ally. It is her job. She is payrolled by HMG. She is a spy, a spook, a Recruit - a saviour of the civilised world.

She has cultivated contacts under the guise of needing munitions and explosives; she has seduced fanatics with her lies, and her lies about lies, and she has established her connection to their networks. Now she feeds them information – about ways in which counter-terrorism services operate. All this she has supposedly learnt from her time as an eco-warrior, as an anarchist. They will use anyone for their purpose and, whilst she remains useful to them, all is well. But she is playing dangerous game and is well aware of that fact.

Now she is solo, a rebel, a renegade, living on the edge of the thrill, full of adrenaline and more in control of her own life than she has ever been before.

She was left for dead by the roadside . That was not supposed to happen. They were supposed to be kidnapped together – that was the plan. Something had gone wrong. By the time she was able to make her way to Mogadishu, both Harriet and Jennifer were dead – killed in an botched rescue attempt by the Kenyan Security Forces. No information had been obtained about the whereabouts of the small carved ebony box, the one she had more than once seen Harriet studying.

A week later Harriet's house was ransacked. Amongst her papers they found nothing of obvious interest – just a photograph of a cottage surrounded by roses. It was nothing but it meant something to Katrina.

Katrina is in London. She has come in on a regular flight to Heathrow. She is wearing her dark-green *hijab* and using one of her several British passports, but it is not one supplied by HMG, though it rings no alarm bells as she enters the country.

Two days later a bomb is detonated in a busy market in North London, killing five people and injuring dozens more, many seriously.

~

At a high-level meeting of government ministers, heads of the Intelligence and Counter-Terrorism Services, Erasmus explains his strategy. It is not short-term – though he highlights some quick wins – and it is not infallible. But it most certainly *is* necessary.

When the meeting was over he returned to his new desk overlooking the Thames. There was work to be done. The threat had come home to roost. Katrina was one of their own – had been one of their own. But somewhere out there she had taken a turning that no one else had noticed. The signs had been missed until it was too late.

Now he must prepare to confront a new breed of terrorist. One that is neither fervent convert nor ecstatic prophet, nor delusional dictator. No, one far more dangerous and devious still. A rogue agent, an apostate, a heretic without conscience. One their own. None more callously disinterested than Katrina al-Kadassa.

48. UK

It was mid-July and the phoney war before a September election was well underway. Since the introduction of five-year terms Parliament had become predictably unpredictable, with general elections always held in May, unless there were exceptional circumstances, of course.

The present Home Secretary, standing in at Prime Minister's Question Time on this particular Wednesday, was clearly out of her depth. She appreciated the irony that economic immigrants' children were becoming radicalised. However, her attempt to find a middle road in managing immigration had only succeeded in alienating her supporters for its ineffectiveness and aggravating her opponents for her intransigence.

The liberal debate surrounding tolerance, and the need to be on guard against intolerance, had imploded. It was realised by the liberal intelligentsia, perhaps too late, that intolerance cannot be tolerated; it is a fundamental contradiction, in a society which adheres to liberal values, that to wage a necessary war requires the suspension of some individual liberties, for the common good, lest those liberties be lost forever. This was the premise of mobilisation in the Second World War and the fight against Nazi Germany; somehow it had been forgotten.

Into the whirling maelstrom of these times of dangerous uncertainty, into the political and moral confusion of a society torn between very different religious premises and cultural views – where values were hijacked by sociopaths for their personal satisfaction and the achievement of total power – into this great storm stepped the calming influence of Anthony Miller, newly elected Leader of Her Majesty's Opposition, a sinner among men, a force of will - in this unnatural time of ignorance and terror. The new Leader of the Opposition was now in full flight.

"Racial warfare among and between different minority ethnic groups is rife. Our own children are travelling abroad to fight for Al Shabad and ISAL – wherever there is the opportunity to fight against the so called unbeliever. The UK is leaking like a sieve. Everyday young men, women, and children are travelling abroad and crossing over the border into Syria. Parents are holding up their hands in horror, seemingly unable to do anything about it. The irony that their children, brought up in a western culture that allows – now even expects – its youth to rebel, is not lost on us. What, may I ask, is the Government doing to stop this?"

～

The BBC was interviewing people for the popular weekly social history program *Last Words*. Emily Smythe was visiting an old man in a nursing home in Surrey.

"When we were young, the War was not a distant memory; we played in its shadow. There were no ethnic minorities, only people. Our friends were Catholics, and Jews, and lads from the council estate and girls from the big houses across the road. We lived under a cloud that was shaped like a mushroom, but we didn't care. We saw them shoot JFK and drop napalm in Vietnam, and we heard the music of freedom. We were young. But now – what is this? What is this country? Look what we have become in our desire for material wealth where the weakest goes to the wall and a *why-should-I-care?* attitude is the norm. No, this is not my country. It is a hollow replica, a grotesque caricature of itself. The good years have gone and now we are only waiting to die."

His hand trembled as he stretched for his cup of tea and took a sip. When he put it down it was time to sleep again.

～

Inspector Erasmus was perfectly aware that, if he were to play a part in the battle for civilisation, then he would not be able to write history on his own.

He would require assistance. His authorial counterpart was, apparently, busy judging at the Hay-on-Wye Literary Festival, and there was no other obvious candidate to assist him. He needed another angle, a different approach. He decided to call Wetherton to see if he would be willing to help further in some as yet undefined way.

Peter Wetherton was on extended leave, waiting to be called to a hearing of the Police Complaints Commission. He had observed events first hand at the riot in Hackney and was a key witness. He had also suffered two broken ribs and was recuperating before returning to duty. He was getting bored. His wife was getting tired of him under her feet, but the doctor would not let him return to work. Erasmus' offer seemed like an unexpected ray of sunlight, dispelling the gloom and frustration. Wetherton jumped at the opportunity, hurting his ribs as he did so.

"Now you won't necessarily be investigating the case directly," Erasmus explained, "more often you will be crafting something, shaping a plan, plotting a direction or completing a thought. I need your unique perspective on things."

"That's fine by me," replied Wetherton, "I'm more than happy to assist in any way I can – sounding board, investigator, secretary, journalist – anything that's needed!"

"Well I hope journalist won't be necessary!" he replied.

～

Anthony Miller was indeed a force of nature. His rise to political power had been meteoric. This was not due simply to the vacuum that existed – though that was of course a contributory factor – but because he was blessed with the gift of certainty in his own ability, his own self-belief, and his own destiny. He was not tainted by feelings of weakness; he was a man who dealt only with challenges and certainties; he knew nothing of problems or doubts.

His popularity, across the traditional political spectrum, was difficult to account for, but whatever the reason he exploited the fact to the full. To the humble wife he was a caring soul; to the working man he was salt of the earth; to the educated professional he was intelligent and reasonable. Only the old establishment, with its dislike of the new and its disdain for the self-made man, begged to differ.

Personally I found him rather impressive, as any man of discernment might. But I also found him perhaps a bit too sure of himself, on occasion. This would sometimes border on arrogance, as when he confronted the Nationalists on independence, or when he tackled the London strikes in the brutal way that he did. Still, I could not help but admire the man - at least, that was the case to begin with.

49. PM

When Anthony Miller became Prime Minister in August, his focus was
not so much on the wars in the Middle East, Africa, and Afghanistan,
but rather those on the home front. This was in direct contrast to previous
government policies of maintaining multiple conflicts abroad, well away
from our own shores. Anthony Miller did not see his mission in
messianic terms, though others might. He viewed it more practically.
The longer-term effort must be to win hearts and minds but, for the time
being, he needed quick victories. The terrorist cells in the UK that seemed
to have sprung up spontaneously - he needed to disrupt them and he
needed to locate the unseen controlling figures behind each and every
act of terrorism. He must be more radical still in order to fight the forces
that threatened democracy's very existence, to fight both as a nation and
as individuals. Anthony Miller, although he did not see himself as an
avenging angel, accepted the task that had fallen to him as if it were the
Will of God, though he himself would not have claimed such authority.
He believed it was quite unnecessary to believe anything beyond the
means to an end.

Anthony Miller's new government was wasting no time in setting
about its business. That business was to address head-on the conflicts
that were now spilling out onto the streets in an ever-increasing spiral of
violence, from the food riots in Bristol to the looting in Oxford, and the
sporadic violence in the East End. The new Home Secretary appeared on
national television:

"Society is at breaking point; the multicultural experiment has failed
and is imploding into a war of the gated middle classes and the riotous
under classes, the striped lawns of the suburbs and the brutal concrete
of the urban ghettos. Extreme groups are ever more successful in their

indoctrination of young people, who seem ill-equipped to resist. Their emotional and psychological dependency on social media, with its immediate and often unconsidered communication, seems to render them incapable of thinking for themselves."

Apocalyptic addresses, such as this, were becoming ever more frequent. The Home Secretary's rhetoric was close to that of the PM and clearly of the same school. There was even talk of ordering the Army onto the streets and imposing martial law. A huge vacuum was appearing and the normal democratic processes seemed incapable of replenishing it with anything but an increasingly toxic atmosphere. Would society dissolve into a period of anarchy before one interest triumphed over another? Who would haul themselves from the wreckage of civilisation and take power?

Anthony Miller, the new British Prime Minister, realised the harsh necessities of *realpolitik*. He had reinforced the UK's borders against the waves of migrants flooding across Europe from the war-torn Middle East and Africa. The Royal Navy was not only patrolling but also preventing migrant crossings, in the English Chanel and the North Sea. The UK was well beyond an Australian style response to the refugee crisis. Its borders were now closed. With a total population approaching eighty million and people living on the streets, with an extreme shortage of housing, there was no more room. The drawbridge was up and the gates were closed.

Anthony Miller, chief among sinners, was not from the start a career politician. His interests had been eclectic – in the arts as an impresario for new pop bands; in industry as an entrepreneur developing digital applications; in journalism as the editor of an underground magazine supporting gay rights – and all he touched seemed to turn to gold. He was courted, flattered, and seduced by the elder statesmen of a particular political party. In due course he beguiled them and was elected their leader. Where he could, he made friends; where he could not, he cultivated enemies to the extent that he was able to predict their hostile moves and circumvent them. He possessed the virtue of self-belief and the vice of total certainty. He was an unnatural force of nature, a sociopath. And as he rose to the top of the great mire he took with him the great majority of the British voting public. There was not a city nor a borough nor a county nor a shire, that did not lend him majority support. His landslide victory empowered him to contemplate undreamt of and extreme solutions; it gave him the most powerful negotiating hand with his European and American allies alike. He could virtually dictate his own terms.

A man is best known by his actions, be they the result of thinking, based on core values, or the lazy result of prejudice. Anthony Miller's actions matched his rhetoric. He was conceited. He was as decisive as he was convinced of his rectitude. Yet everyone – desirous of a saviour – seemed willing to overlook these flaws. Well, almost everyone.

The PM made changes according to the popular mood, using opportunities to reduce civil liberties in certain areas and espouse liberal philosophy in others: detention without charge under terrorism laws was extended whilst freedom of individual expression was encouraged, especially in public life. The fashion for no-platforming, where persons holding views deemed unacceptable or offensive are barred from speaking in public, was eviscerated. He also made other changes, which seemed innocent enough at the time, but prefigured more sinister developments. By seizing more direct power himself, and by marginalising key cabinet colleagues, as well as the opposition, he positioned himself in readiness for dealing with the growing threats in society, especially those that came from abroad, but also those that derived from homegrown indoctrination and the digital grooming of impressionable youths in all sections of society, not merely the underclass or the fundamentalists.

50. Wetherton

Peter Wetherton was an interesting character – not by any means what one might expect of a career policeman. I say interesting because, like Erasmus, he was by no means an exemplar of orthodoxy. His approach to matters was factual and evidence-based – some would say thoroughly scientific - but it was more than that; it was as if he had a peculiar talent for being in the right place at the right time, as on this particular occasion. His anti-terrorism training had seen him working in close co-operation with MI5 and he had made useful contacts there. I shall not describe his aquiline nose and piercing blue eyes, etc. You can imagine his appearance for yourself. Suffice to say his appearance is not his character, nor his motivation, nor his core values - not his whole moral being – as you will see for yourself.

Since their rendezvous at Somerset House, Erasmus had been in touch with Wetherton once again. They had agreed that Peter should come down to the coast at the weekend. They could have lunch together and perhaps take a stroll together along the beach. There was a fine spot for marsh harriers and, if lucky, they might catch a glimpse of a water rail. Wetherton was a keen birdwatcher – though not a twitcher by any means. He explained the important distinction to Erasmus:

"I merely take my binoculars with me on a walk. Sometimes my walk is designed to take in one or two favourable spots, but that is never my sole purpose. Now the twitcher is a different beast entirely!"

"How so?" enquired Erasmus, interested to know.

"The twitcher is someone who is willing to travel – indeed is *driven* to do so – from one end of the country to the other on hearing that there has been a sighting of a rare bird, usually a migrant that's been blown off course. He (or more rarely She) will have all the requisite gear, including telescope and high-powered cameras with telephoto lenses – a huge financial investment made in support of their hobby or, as I would say, their obsession."

"I see," said Erasmus. Well, now we are here I'm sure you will take advantage of the opportunity to see what there is to be seen – and you must educate me too."

"I'd be delighted!"

Just then a black-headed gull screamed above their heads as another tried to steal a scrap from its beak. This gave Wetherton the excuse to expound upon the several different types of seagull that they were likely to see in the area.

"Look Peter, this isn't going to be straightforward, I can tell you that now," began Erasmus, as he sketched out his approach.

"I understand that – no problem as far as I'm concerned," Wetherton replied, "just point me in the right direction!"

"I think we need to be looking in a different direction from everyone else, pre-empting the new danger, not simply dealing with the current crisis. And it will come, as a consequence, mark my words!"

Erasmus was untypically agitated; it seemed as if something had got under his skin. Wetherton noticed and moved on:

"I'll certainly bear it in mind but, for the moment, what is it we need to do?" he asked.

I presume you have heard of Katrina Al-Kadassa, or Katrina Gordon, as she was known previously? She was one of ours; now she belongs to no one but herself. She has rejected her adopted heritage and the heritage of her father. She is now fuelling the fire without allegiance to any ideology, other than her own personal creed. We need to find her. We need to know what she knows, who she knows. We need to get close to her.

"I see. So what is it you think I can do?"

Erasmus did not answer immediately but then he said:

"I'm not exactly sure. I need to bounce some ideas off you. Do you mind?"

"No, of course not. That's fine."

They walked on along the shingle with the wind gusting occasionally from the south-west. To their right was a scrape raised in the middle of a small lagoon. Wetherton pointed out the curious avocets as they filtered for food with their strangely upcurved bills.

~

About a week later Wetherton got back in touch with Erasmus. He had been working on a plan to reel in the target. It was now ready to be put into action, if Erasmus agreed. It was a simple plan, as are all the best ones. Peter Wetherton would himself would act as a go-between, a fixer, a broker. He would arrange a meeting and an exchange between Erasmus and Katrina. He would use Katrina's MI5 training to enable them to make contact.

But Wetherton was unaware of other forces at work in the story and, despite the possible effectiveness of his plan on one level, on another it was merely superficial. Nonetheless it was permitted to proceed as it might serve a useful narrative purpose. If it did so then it would be justified.

51. Katrina

Katrina al Kadassa receives the report of the abortive raid at Thermopylae. She realises that the girl must have what she wants. Now she knows that she doesn't have it; she has already given it to Erasmus. Katrina left her still alive, deliberately, as a warning.

Katrina is no longer in the UK She has slipped away without any fuss and is relaxing somewhere in Switzerland, near the German border. She plays tennis in the mornings with a Russian girl, whose much older partner prefers to watch, rather than join in. His viewing is often interrupted by business calls. These he would usually deal with sitting at his table under a sunshade but, occasionally, he gets up and moves away, as if the matter were too confidential. By the pool, in the afternoons, she joins the bathing set and alternates refreshing swims with sunbathing. She notices a middle-aged man busy writing at a table in the far corner, thoroughly intent upon what he is doing. Occasionally he takes a break from his work and goes for a dip in the pool. He is not unhandsome,

She realised that she was intrigued by this man's dedication to his task. He was in place every morning by ten o'clock and worked through till lunchtime at one o'clock. He had coffee served at a quarter past eleven and would occasionally look up from his work as if pondering something or searching for a word. He reminded her of someone. She imagined he might be writing his latest best-seller, sweeping his reach across Europe and the Middle East and into Africa, drawing from the darkness of men's hearts, their most powerful passions, and their deepest deceits. An expert in isolation and alienation, he was creating a world in which evil prevailed.

Katrina was waiting. She had nothing to do but wait. She was becoming restless, as she knew she would. She was drawn towards the man at the table who, every day, would set to work writing his book.

She was curious, like an avocet. She wanted to know more. She needed to know more. This irresistible and foolish desire gnawed away at her resolve. Her reading material was dull and uninteresting. Her access to the internet afforded no respite from the tediousness that assaulted her with increasing frequency. She had never been very good at sitting still, and it was no different now, except that she had a reason to do so, rather than being commanded by someone else.

Her independence was hard fought. It had been achieved against a complex web of lies and deceit woven by others and by herself. She had been recruited at Oxford, partly on the basis of her heritage. But her heritage wasn't in question; her allegiance was. She had been the first to question this and, so well trained was she, that no one else seemed to notice – certainly not her controller. At first she had revelled in the inner freedom that her own secret life gave her. Then she had realised that her adherence to a specific radical ideology was as unsavoury as her subjugation to MI5. Her individualism and sense of her own identity were too strong for either cage to hold her for long; now she had forged a new freedom, of her own making.

〜

It is two a.m. and she remains blissfully unaware that he is writing about her. She has no way of knowing. Were she to know she would be both outraged and delighted. She is fast asleep but is not dreaming. She is not dreaming of her father, of her allegiance to no one, of her trip to the beach, when she is no more than four at the most, and her mother is helping her eat an ice cream as it melts in her hand. Later she will dream of playing tennis with a beautiful girl who becomes Harriet and speaks in Italian. It is two a.m. and he is writing about her.

〜

For Katrina this was a family affair, a matter of honour. She wanted what she considered to be her birthright; others might have argued she had already foregone any right she may have once had, by reason of her treachery. Katrina did not consider herself a traitor, nor a hero, nor a martyr. She was exerting her free will; she was under no one else's control. That was her sole intention, without regard to the judgement of others. If she believed anything, she believed that it was her right to live her life as she wished, without subjugating herself to the expectations of others, whatever their culture, religion or politics. Her anarchism was of her own making, was unique, and belonged to no one else. Now she must take back what had been stolen from her.

~

It is surprisingly easy to enter the UK on the Eurostar. She has done it before and will most likely do so again. Paddington Station is a familiar landmark to her, as it is to thousands of others. Just along the road, towards Euston Station, the British Library boasts its presence with a modern mound of architecturally sculpted bricks. Perhaps she could draw him to her here? But she knows he must be searching for her already; she must not be impatient. Meanwhile she should just go about her business as usual.

Although the evening paper made much of the ongoing troubles in the East End of London, she saw no signs of it in the centre of the city or the West End. This was patrolled by police who did not appear to be carrying weapons. Tourists would still stop them and ask for directions and they would still give them. It was all rather quaint and old-fashioned. It was only when she headed out towards Whitechapel that she saw the aftermath of the recent rioting: a burnt-out church; sectarian slogans; shop fronts smashed. The streets were oddly quiet. Armed police were visible on street corners, hovering obviously in groups of half a dozen or so.

She was dressed in a traditional *kurta* and headscarf, with dark coloured *shalwar*. She became a local Bangladeshi or Somalian woman, carrying a plastic bag with shopping. Even she was surprised by her invisibility. The police seemed to be on the lookout for gangs of youths and men. There were a few other women going about their business –

two had stopped to chat – but all the children must be at school or at home. There was an acrid smell in the air that came from the burnt vehicles, especially the plastic interiors; this mixed with other nasty smells emanating from the sewers. The routine maintenance of this part of the capital's infrastructure was probably off schedule. She passed the women talking together but she could not understand what they were saying. She spoke only her native tongue, English, with just a little Arabic that enabled her to get by. As far as Urdu, or Punjabi, or Polish were concerned she was completely lost, like most people in this country, she imagined. Nevertheless her disguise was sufficient to allow her to pass through these streets undetected. Eventually she reached her destination, a dull metal door off a side street that opened outwards when she unclasped the padlock, revealing a flight of stairs up to a first floor flat. This was a safe house, one of her own. She would not be here long.

She had brought with her some fresh supplies but most of what she needed was already stored in tins in cupboards in the small kitchen, thanks to Dorothy – she would call her later. She remembered a squat she had visited once in Paris and felt almost as if she were in a palace by comparison. There had been floorboards missing, intermittent cold water, and cockroaches. This place was clean and the plumbing and electricity both worked. Next she reclaimed her laptop from the bottom of the wardrobe in the single bedroom. She hacked into a nearby Internet Café's Wi-Fi and spoofed her IP address - a standard precaution. Anyone trying to track her activity would be misdirected across several continents before arriving back in a different part of London entirely, on the north bank of the Thames. Once this was done she was able to relax and think about her personal needs: bathroom, a cup of tea, a decent meal. As she came out of the bathroom a cat rubbed against her legs. It was a local stray that she had taken in sometimes – it had most probably come in through the kitchen window which she had left ajar when filing the kettle. It looked at her, as if knowingly, and seemed to smile as it purred.

After she had fed the cat and eaten her dinner, she washed up and cleared things away, put the laptop on the small kitchen table and settled down to work. She needed to find out more about Inspector Erasmus and to do so she needed to gain access to the new National ID database. Her passwords would be out of date and certainly set off alarms. She had to be more resourceful than that, and she was. She had previously used the account of her controller, Marston, to set up a hidden gateway. This established an access portal that was untraceable to any individual person, either official or civilian. Once used she could burn the trace of any search activity. This was achieved by a logic trap she had hidden in an update trigger in the database that invoked a call to a standard stored-procedure, whose method ensured the automatic audit trail was wiped. She had, at the same time as planting this code, amused herself with modifying the North West Rail timetabling system. She had made sure that trains from London to Birmingham would be required to stop at any station of her choice, on receipt of a coded text message from a mobile phone. This was simply showing off but she thought it might be useful one day – an arbitrary contingency for an unexpected circumstances.

Travelling always made Katrina both tired and alert simultaneously, whether or not it involved crossing time zones. The one thing she didn't seem to have in her bag, or anywhere in the flat, were sleeping pills. She made a short trip down to the all-night chemist to buy some. It was gone nine-thirty in the evening and the streets were deserted; she was glad to get back to the flat without seeing anyone.

She had set herself up as a free agent – some would say mercenary – providing services to the highest bidder. She always negotiated her own deals and made use, without conscience, of friends, colleagues, and acquaintances to suit her own purposes. She had assumed she would continue in this line of business only until she had recovered her inheritance from the interfering Erasmus, but now she found she was beginning to like her work, more and more.

As part of her training as an agent with MI5, she had learnt many of the standard, and non-standard, ways of doing things. One of the habits she had learnt and retained was a standard communications protocol using a major national online broadsheet. The obituary columns were especially useful for this purpose – standard structure and format, common phrases, dates and times of funerals etc. All that was needed was a name – a code name. This was given two names above the obituary containing the details of a meeting. The message was from someone mentioned in the following obituary, usually the person placing the notice. This was how Katrina received a contact message from 'P.W.' She did not know who P.W. was but the demise of a 'Mr. J. Erasmus' caught her attention and, two places above, her own MI5 code name. Someone was trying to arrange a meeting with her.

Katrina called Dorothy. Dorothy had a permanent crush on Katrina, who deliberately kept her at arms-length, most of the time. Dorothy was ever eager to please. She understood what she had to do.

Two days later a taxi cab drew up outside Highgate Cemetery and a lady in black stepped out and walked towards the Karl Marx monument. An odd shrine to find in the heart of the capital of Capitalism. She wore black gloves and carried in her left hand a small black book, like a bible. She walked past the man kneeling by a grave on her left and stopped at another grave some twenty yards further on. There was an elderly woman walking her small dog – maybe a Highland Terrier – and a female gardener in a Hi Vis jacket, clearing around the headstones with a noisy strimmer. She paid her respects for a few minutes then turned and walked away past the man she had noticed previously. As she passed him she glanced back – it was the merest motion but he read it instantly. The man followed her out of the cemetery where she was standing and waiting for him.

He introduced himself: "I'm Witherspoon, Peter Witherspoon," he said, holding out his hand. She ignored the gesture.

"What do you want?" she asked.

"Well, I think it's more a question of what you want. I have some information – about something that belongs to you. I think I can help you get it back."

"I see. And I am to trust your word on this, I suppose?"

"You don't have to – here, take this."

He drew a ring from his pocket and held it for her to see.

"So, you recognise it then?"

"Of course I do! Why do you have it?"

"It's a token, a gesture if you like."

"How much?"

"My client is a reasonable man – let's say twenty percent of the final holdings."

"Very well, but not here. I will contact you."

And so saying she turned and walked off to where her taxi was waiting. She recognised his type – the worst of the Secret Service's lackeys, no class, a wide-eyed barrow boy.

Peter was pleased that his plan had been successful, so far. Yes, they could have picked her up here and now but that would have been premature. They needed to learn more. This way they would be able to keep her in sight, as long as they had what she wanted.

The gardener stopped strimming and, taking the strap off her shoulder, put the heavy tool down beside her. She picked up a flask, opened it, and poured herself a cup of sweet tea. She watched as the man followed the woman towards the gate. She would learn later from Dorothy exactly what P.W. had said to her.

~

Before Katrina was able to organise another meeting she received confirmation of an important commission, one that she had come to London for specifically. She would have to leave the country for about a week or ten days. She realised this could work to her advantage. She would be on neutral territory and this would remove any advantage Witherspoon's client may have – that is to say, any advantage Erasmus might have, for he was undoubtedly the client.

The next day she was on a plane out of Gatwick and heading for Geneva, from where she would take a coach to Lausanne. She was travelling light, with only hand luggage. Dorothy had sent a suitcase ahead to the hotel where she was staying. Dorothy would join her later. She would have her reward.

52. John

John possessed more power than he had originally expected. After all, he was engaged in the writing of a story and had deliberately chosen to introduce himself from the perspective of another character. This gave him substance and confirmed his existence to the Reader. As he wrote this observation down he chuckled quietly to himself – he was both within the story and without.

His Parish Priests, who heard Martin Hogg's confessions, were different each time – one-off contracts – and his own 'twin' was an unknown and typically out of work actor. This sleight of hand pleased him. He knew it would only delay Erasmus, but it bought him time, time to prepare.

He had not always been a writer, had never set out to be a writer, and only became involved in writing as a means to an end. He needed to earn a living. Of course, there was no guarantee he would do so, but he was creating an image, a myth, a new history for himself, a new identity. It was as if he needed to become someone else in order to disappear and in order to re-exist. He knew that, in this mode, he would become a person of interest and that he was likely to be sought by his detective. His earlier attempt to supply a stand-in Author had succeeded, up to a point, but Erasmus had now got beyond that particular subterfuge and seen it for what it was – a temporary ruse. He was a worthy opponent, a gifted detective, and a curious one too. It was certainly his curiosity that had led him this far. Equally John's authority and imagination had made this possible. They were most definitely well-matched.

As he sat at his writing table by the pool, John realised he was being watched – studied almost. At first he did not recognise his stalker, but then she moved and he caught a glimpse of a look on her face that reminded him of someone he had seen before, in an entirely different place and time. It was when he had been at an anti-Austerity rally in London – a mishmash of likely and unlikely protestors and protest groups. He was studying it, like a predator studies its prey. He was researching subject matter for his new book. Yes, it was definitely her. She was some sort of green activist. She did not see that he had noticed her and he was careful to show no sign he was aware she had been watching him.

~

It is two a.m. and he is writing about Katrina. She has no way of knowing. Were she to know, she would be both outraged and delighted. She is fast asleep and is not yet dreaming. She is not dreaming of her father, of her allegiance to no one, of her trip to the beach, when she is no more than four at the most, and her mother is helping her eat an ice cream as it melts in her hand. It is two a.m. and he is writing about her.

He has no way of knowing what she is dreaming, or what she will dream, but he could decide – were he to choose to do so. He notices that his foot is painful. It may be cramp or gout, he is not sure, but takes an ibuprofen tablet anyway. He knows he will be discovered, that he will be revealed as the Author but he is not concerned. He has had time to prepare for this; he has had time to think about it; he has had time to live another life before any of this ever happened, and is happy to have done so. But now he must sleep, for tomorrow will be a busy day. He will soon be meeting face to face with his – or someone's – creation, an Inspector Julian Erasmus, a character who has insisted on becoming real, on pursuing his investigations beyond the normal boundaries of a nominal murder enquiry, and who has established his own operating parameters. John has no power to deny him, as he has no choice but to play the role of Author. He has entered his own narrative and this he must do to solve the mystery he has created – but he cannot guarantee that he will.

~

Of course, John has placed himself by the pool. He is by the pool, and he is not. He is certainly writing – this is proof of that. He has placed himself by the pool because that is where he needs to be, where they all need to be, in due course. It is by the pool they will eventually meet. It is curious, but John suspects Katrina has more to say than she is telling. He waits. He waits for her to make her move, and he waits for Erasmus to arrive, as he sits by the pool writing. He knows he will come. And he knows that unexpected events are about to occur of which he has no specific knowledge, only a general impression.

After lunch John usually takes a short siesta – half an hour, no more. He will then take a walk down to the lake and back. He likes to establish these routines, if only so that he can occasionally break them in an act of existential defiance. He is certainly self-disciplined and knows he cannot neglect his work, if he is to finish it. Although he is working to no publisher's deadline, he has set one for himself. The work will be finished within the month. If this seems ambitious then it is also a question of concentration and holding in front of him the picture and the movement, the story, he is creating. Its consistency, its continuity, its coherence – all these depend upon his mastery, his stamina, and his stubbornness. Driven only by his own desire for completion. He will finish, he must finish. But for the moment he must remain patient, reserving his energies and saving his strength.

He has been struggling to realise the denouement of the plot, recalling what Jennifer had suggested about not providing one, and how this would be cheating the Reader of their rightfully expected pleasure. I can say this with a degree of certainty. It is a common problem among writers. A writer is also a reader, but a reader who must discover for the first time where the story leads. Of course this is every reader's experience, in some way, but it must always remain secondary. The reader's imagination recreates the scene that was first created by the writer. John is feeling his way towards what will be. The ideas are beginning to arrive from all around and to arrange themselves in juxtaposition and in sequence. He is beginning to understand the measure of his own work. He is desperate to let the story tell itself, without overexertion or too much control on his part. He is learning to write what wishes to be written, what insists on being written.

Now John is waiting. We know who he is waiting for. We may think we know why – perhaps we do. But others are, as yet, unaware, and they will need to realise before matters can be resolved. Erasmus, for example, has as yet no knowledge of this splendid pool in this beautiful location.

53. Erasmus

When Martin left the Globe he went straight to confession. Erasmus waited a few minutes and then left too. There was no need to try and follow, one of Evans' men would be tailing him.

The next time they met was in St Pauls, on the opposite bank of the Thames. Curiously Martin went to the confessional booth straight after their meeting – I say curiously because on the previous occasion it had been a Catholic Church. He had not thought of his counterpart, the author of this work, as being devout or religious in any particular way.

Erasmus picked up the trail a few days later, again after one of their brief meetings. Evans' man followed him, this time to St Martin-in-the-Fields. Erasmus slipped into the seats at the back of the church. There was only one other person present, a woman dressed all in black, whom he did not recognise. Then the priest came out of the vestry and entered the confessional booth. About two minutes later he exited and shortly after Martin came out too. He halted in front of the altar and crossed himself. Then he went and sat next to the woman in black. They sat together for at least five minutes before Erasmus slipped away again.

Erasmus had seen enough of this story: Martin was a stand-in, a substitute, a deceiving doppelganger. It would be necessary for him to continue the charade of their occasional meetings but he would use them to his own advantage. He would feed his own misdirection into the equation. Whoever it was pulling the strings and whispering behind the curtain would be revealed soon enough.

~

Wetherton had returned from his meeting at the cemetery. Erasmus could not be certain but it seemed Katrina was using the same double in both deceptions: the young woman in black. Wetherton had not expected al Kadassa herself to appear – he had expected a go-between. But what piqued Erasmus' interest was the possibility that the same person was being deployed by both Katrina and the Author. This was a link that cast an entirely different light on things. It was as if there was the possibility of both of them – Katrina as well as himself – having an existence outside of the story. He had expected the Author to exist in both domains, but only now did it seem to make sense that at least one other character might be so strongly defined and motivated as to attain the same complex existential duality.

Wherever she had been at the time, Wetherton was meeting her go-between in the cemetery, and al Kadassa would not have been far away. She would have been watching them. He knew she was in the country. But when Wetherton received a message saying she had gone abroad again, he was disappointed.

"Do we know where?" he asked.

"No, I'm afraid not," replied Wetherton, "but we suspect she's still somewhere on the Continent."

"Let me know as soon as you hear anything definite."

"Of course," Wetherton replied. Erasmus was disappointed he would not be able to pursue his original plan. Instead, he immediately started to adapt it to fit the new circumstances.

∼

Erasmus had been too busy recently to keep up with the news but even he was aware that matters were steadily worsening across the country. He turned on the television to watch *Newsnight*. A Professor of Political Sociology was pronouncing on the state of the nation. He was questioned impartially, and with rather too much deference, by an inquisitor clearly out of his depth and by no means on a par with his far more illustrious predecessors:

"The traditional north/south divide has become overlaid with a rural/urban divide. The multiculturalism of the cities is made up of densely packed working- class populations rubbing up against each other on a daily basis. In the Shires the integration happens on a smaller scale but more effectively. Added to this are the non-relativistic and non-pluralistic teachings of the newly vibrant religious cliques – people are seeking answers to the problems of our times and not finding those answers in political discourse, which has become detached from, and alienating to, the general population. Traditions of freedom and tolerance are being swamped by extremes of populism and absolutism."

A discussion panel pursued this thesis, to and fro, as if immune from the reality of events. The debate turned to the destruction of ancient historical sites – cultural vandalism, a new Dark Ages. The pillaging of these sites by imperial powers in earlier centuries was now a fortunate act of preservation. At the same time this made museums potential targets under the extreme ideology of fanatical jihadists.

"Do you believe that the Louvre or the British Museum, for example, might be targeted?" asked the interviewer.

"I would say that is certain," declared the Professor, "the irony is that these people are in fact selling looted historical artefacts on the black market. So at the same time as condemning and destroying these symbols of 'pagan' religion, they are using them to fund their own cause."

"There is a solution, I believe," interjected another member of the panel, a military specialist:

"We have the ability to take out the enemy without destroying these world heritage sites. We could use a neutron bomb. This will leave the sites intact, killing only the enemy."

Another member of the panel responded:

"Perhaps the best 'nuclear option' is to destroy the sites ourselves – obliterate them using conventional bombs – and then to disrupt and destroy the trade in these goods."

This suggestion met with a degree of approval. In the light of the absolute harm to humanity being perpetrated by ISAL and its affiliated groups, perhaps it was necessary to think and to do the hitherto inconceivable. There was no room for the honourable 'Colonel Blimp' approach to war.

The debate turned to the question of British citizens travelling to join ISAL. As well as young men of fighting age, there were also young women, with families, who wished to be part of a new caliphate. Given that allegiance to ISAL was allegiance to sworn enemies of the state and, indirectly, threatened the position and person of our King, was this not treason? The Panel was inconclusive on this issue but seemed to agree that the multicultural experiment had not succeeded in integrating large groups of society into pre-existing British culture. Instead they had retained their distinctiveness in effective isolation, at a cost to the nation's wellbeing.

Someone raised the question of returning UK citizens, once ISAL had been defeated, but this was considered premature; 'cross that bridge if and when we get to it' was the consensus.

~

Erasmus got up and poured himself a drink. The whisky warmed and relaxed him. He knew that were he to drink in company he would most likely become morose and then belligerent. It was best to drink his whisky alone – and it lasted longer that way. He recalled from a previous investigation, in which the MoD had 'enlisted' his help, the strange traditions of the Officers' Mess. He had never understood their bonhomie – but then again:

"Ave, Imperator, morituri te salutant" might well have been their motto. He wondered what went through the minds of people facing death, and those suicide bombers who embraced it with a vengeance. Were the Islamist fanatics merely an example of another death cult?

He turned the programme off. He could not solve the problem, interested though he was. An individual has an individual's limitations. He had finished his whisky. It was time for bed.

The following morning he was woken early by a call from Wetherton. They had located Katrina al Kadassa. She was in Switzerland, staying at an expensive hotel on the shores of *Lac Leman*.

The Author would be there too, in Switzerland. Although he had no specific clue or actual evidence to support this conclusion, he knew it implicitly. It was not consistent with any internal logic. Nevertheless, he was as sure as if he were the Author himself – it is precisely what he would have done.

He would like to have talked to someone about this – to check his idea. But Wetherton, useful ally and confidant that he was, could not help him on this occasion. He realised this and did not ask him. Instead he turned to his own resources.

He set off to walk past the Cathedral to the railway station – having persuaded Cheshire not to follow him beyond the bridge, or so he believed – he pondered his next move. Sometimes he found that a brisk walk would stimulate those difficult-to-wake brain cells that held vital clues to an investigation. He reasoned that Katrina al Kadassa would be set and ready for his arrival. He suspected that the Author had been biding his time and was also prepared. No matter if he had lost the element of surprise, he had at least tracked them down and they were no longer dancing haphazardly across time and space; they were no longer merely imagined beings but had substance and motive. Their mutual instantiation was almost complete.

~

Erasmus had booked a direct flight to Geneva with Norwegian Airlines. He would be picked up at the airport by a courtesy car. He was at Gatwick a good two hours ahead of departure. He decided to browse through the top 20 paperbacks in W.H. Smith's. He started to read the blurb on the back of one – a former prize-winner. Then he opened the book at random to assess the prose – was it readable? Was it pseudo Americana? Was it full of gratuitous expletives? He put it down and selected another. He should not have been surprised, and he wasn't. It was a thriller. It seemed somehow familiar – perhaps he had read it before? He was not sure. He put it down again. But then he changed his mind. It looked promising, though he couldn't say why. Perhaps it was the distinctive cover? He picked it up and took it to the counter. He handed the assistant his passport and boarding card and paid for the book by debit card.

He accepted the free bottle of water but declined the bargain-priced bar of chocolate.

At that moment John was watching the sea eagles over the lake when his mobile beeped, indicating he had a text message. It was a notification that Erasmus had made a purchase at Heathrow airport. He responded to the information service provider and, after a few moments, received confirmation that the same card had recently been used to pay for a flight to Geneva.

Erasmus put the book and the bottle of water into his briefcase, then went back to the lounge to wait for the gate number to appear on the departure board. He had seated himself in sight of a television. The news was reporting that ISAL had beheaded two more western hostages in the new Caliphate. But it seemed to him that the destruction of historical monuments upset people more. Perhaps this was because these objects of ancient civilisations were irreplaceable whereas people are not?

He began to read his book. It definitely seemed oddly familiar. Perhaps he had seen the film dubbed from the French or with subtitles? He checked the departure board; the gate number for his flight was now showing so he began the long walk to the gate, using the travellator, feeling as if he were on less than solid ground. In his mind's eye he had somehow formed an image of the place he was going to visit, for the first time. He could not help it. And he knew that this place would be quite different and not as he had expected. He also knew that he would not know what this image was precisely – it would not come into focus – until he arrived at his destination and was confronted by reality. It was a difference between expectation and actuality, between imagination and reality. He dismissed this line of thought and tried not to develop a picture beforehand. Instead, he cleared his mind by focussing on his breathing. He was on board the aircraft now and the plane had taxied to the end of the runway. The engines began to build power and became terribly loud. Suddenly the plane lurched forward, rapidly gaining speed. His stomach seemed to lurch suddenly towards the ground. At last, after what seemed like an eternity, Erasmus breathed again, calmly and deliberately, as if he were watching himself do so from a great height.

54. President

Anthony Miller PM was in regular contact with his counterpart in Washington. He was keen to exploit the 'special relationship' and to benefit himself as much as possible. One of the first things he had done on being elected was to invite the President of the United States to visit the UK The irresistible temptation of the famous links at the Royal and Ancient Golf Club, at St Andrews, would be certain to persuade him and secure an early visit.

Anthony Miller PM had met the President on one earlier occasion, whilst still in opposition. It was only a brief meeting but the two of them seemed to have hit it off. He had been currying favour with a number of important figures, including useful Wall Street bankers and top academics at MIT. He was looking for what it was that people wanted, what drove them, what they would give their eye teeth for – and he would usually find it. Sometimes he made allies in this way; sometimes he simply made contacts. He always made certain he stayed in touch. The wider his network, the greater his influence.

He had a call with the President scheduled for tonight. He would be working late. The time difference could hardly be more inconvenient, to most people. But Miller was not phased; he enjoyed working all hours – it gave him an advantage. He thrived on exercising his mind and body and, most of all, living on adrenaline. He was never so happy as when engaged in the cut and thrust of intellectual and political skirmishing. Whilst he skirmished he continued to develop his long-term strategy and sought advantage in each individual move along the way.

There was still time for a swim. The building of a basement pool at Number 10 would take another six months – although planning permission had already been fast-tracked by Westminster City Council.

Until then he would have to use a nearby hotel, overlooking the Thames. He slipped out the back of the Number 10, wearing running gear and a hoody. He was listening to Fleetwood Mac's *Rumours* on his headset. His taste in music was certainly eclectic and it also knew few temporal boundaries; he also had Vivaldi and Arty Shaw on his MP3 player.

Anthony Miller's personal bodyguards were detailed not to let the PM out of their sight. They didn't. Not for a minute. If he thought he was incognito and alone, then he was wrong. A couple of runners, a man and a woman, were jogging alongside the Thames. They altered their route to place a tail on him. As he made his way over to St. James' Park, and down across Birdcage Walk, another runner was seen approaching from further to the right. One of the pair, the woman, seemed to alter her course, as if to intercept. But then the errant runner turned and headed away. She changed tack again and rejoined her partner in formation.

After his swim Anthony Miller felt invigorated. He took a cab back to Downing Street. He had seen the runners following him and he knew the taxi was provided courtesy of MI5, but he played along with them. No need to upset protocol. Not just yet. He slipped back into Number 10 through the back garden, where he was greeted by the grinning household cat, and went straight to his study. He had some preparation to do before tonight's telephone call.

The President had spent the day – on and off – trying to persuade his wife that a trip to the UK was more important than her mother's seventieth birthday. He had not succeeded. In the end he played his master card - shopping. Shopping in London. Shopping in Oxford Street and at Harrods. And yes (what have I done!) you can bring your mother too. Affairs of State were indeed a simple matter in comparison to maintaining an equilibrium in the domestic cold war; he needed all his hard-learned political skills to maintain peace on the home front.

His aide found him practising his putting stroke in the Oval Office. The President was preparing for an important overseas trip, one which he could not entrust to the Secretary of State.

"Sir, you are due to make a call to the UK Prime Minister in fifteen minutes."

"Yes, thank you. I guess we'll be using the 'Bat-Phone,' Robin?"

"Yes Sir, the 'Bat-Phone', as you say." Robin Schultzer was used to the joke, and dutifully humoured his Commander in Chief.

"You'll be speaking to The Riddler, Sir? – I mean Mr Miller?"

"Right. No problem. Yeah!" The president had, finally, sunk a putt.

Settled at his desk, some twenty minutes later, Zeb T. Reezan, the President of the United States, waited. Soon the phone would ring and a friendly female voice, with a slight southern drawl, would inform him that she had the Prime Minister of the UK on the line, and would he care to take the call?

He drifted into a reverie: the crowd were all applauding as he approached the final green. He doffed his cap and waved it at the gallery. Then the crowd hushed as he walked to within a few feet of the hole, where his ball had come to a halt after a fine seven-iron shot from slight rough to the right of the green. He lined himself up and took a deep breath, holding himself tight for the put. The ball moved, closer, to the edge, and dropped. The gallery erupted! He threw his cap to the crowd and his wife threw her arms around him!

The phone rang. Would he like to accept (southern drawl) a call from the Prime Minister of the United Kingdom? Damn right he would!

"Put him through," he replied, waving Schultzer out of the Oval Office.

"Hey Tony, how ya doin'?"

"Hi Zeb, I'm good thanks. You too I hope?"

"Why yeah, just fine. Got my handicap down to three last week."

"Well that's terrific. I'll need to practise my swing, I can see!"

∼

When they finished their banter they settled down to what others would consider more serious matters. Of course we may not hear what they had to say; even if we have a certain level of security clearance, we are not members of the FBI nor MI5 (unless of course you are?). Anyway, I think we have heard the most important things they had to say. Perhaps we will join them later, on the Old Course, on the east coast of Fife. If we're lucky we might get to see the Super Tornado jet fighters taking off and landing at RAF Leuchars. I remember that the wind blows there, even on a sunny day, so bring a hat and a warm coat, and maybe a pair of gloves.

55. Coup

Reggie had asked Evans to pop in and see him later that afternoon.
He needed him for an important diplomatic task.

"Ah Ted, come in. Do sit down"

"Thank you Sir," Evans replied. He waited for Reggie to settle himself
back into his chair but, unusually, he remained standing. After a moment
he began:

"You are aware that next month's summit has been brought forward?"

"Yes, though I'm not sure why. But it doesn't really concern me. Does it?"

Reggie had raised an eyebrow and added a smiling frown for
additional effect.

"Well, actually, yes, it does."

"How so?"

"Let me explain." Reggie proceeded to explain that the chap in charge
of Security had slipped up and broken his leg – he laughed at his own
unintended joke – whilst Evans remained po-faced.

"Well, never mind." He continued, "So you see, I need someone to
replace him, and you're my best man – not that I'm getting married
again!" (another unwelcome pun; again no reaction from Evans).

"I'll need to meet the team straightaway."

"Yes, of course. Absolutely. I'll call Johnson in now – he should be
waiting outside."

Johnson, Deputy Head of Security, entered and shook hands with
Evans. They had met once before but neither had made much of the other.
It was a clean start.

～

The European Summit was to be held not far from Geneva at the
beginning of August. That gave Evans less than two weeks to prepare, to

check and test the existing arrangements. It was cutting things fine but he would do the best he could – "always better to have a deadline" he remarked to himself.

Meanwhile COBRA, comprising at present: Prime Minister, Chancellor, and Home Secretary, was planning its strategy. They were encamped at Chequers, the Prime Minister's official country residence, amidst security that was manifestly even tighter than usual. A military protection zone had been established all around a two mile perimeter, and attack helicopters were on standby whilst the new Lightning jet aircraft patrolled an extensive air exclusion zone.

The atmosphere was heated. Even this small number did not find it easy to agree on the details. In some ways hardly surprising given that each one was of a determined and stubborn nature, thick-skinned and adamant – which of course they had to be to reach the high offices they had now attained. They were discussing the position on relations with the major continental players: Germany, Poland, Russia and Switzerland. France was already given over to the new and powerful Islamic leadership and Italy had reverted to a collection of city states. France's capitulation had been done in the name of preserving peace, but it was viewed rather differently by many who sat in their comfy chairs on the other side of La Manche. 'Invasion fever' was not too dramatic a term to describe the fears that were growing in England and Wales - Scotland had its own position on matters but was too much in the grip of its own economic crisis to be able to play much of a part. Northern Ireland had already been ceded to the Irish Republic.

∼

BBC's Chief Political Editor, reporting from Chequers:

"The Cabinet's safety seems assured, here in the haven of Middle England, amidst green fields and hills. And indeed it is. But it is not a terrorist attack they need fear most, it is a political attack; an attack that could come at almost any time and from any direction – even from within their own party. The government whips, their enforcers, will hope to be well on top of things – assuming they are not themselves scheming behind the Prime Minister's back. Nothing is certain in politics but its unpredictability and its ruthlessness."

~

Ted Evans was currently at Sandringham, finalising security arrangements for the Royal Family's visit the following week. Once happy with these, he would get back to Johnson and review arrangements for the European Summit. A few days later he was surprised to see a number of distinguished persons arriving and he requested the King's Equerry to bring him up to date immediately.

The Equerry apologised for any inconvenience but the King had requested a low- profile event.

"Well, it would have been helpful to know beforehand, but we are where we are, so let's do our best," Evans said.

Evans was familiar with the King's preference for autonomy and doing and speaking as he wished – this should have been no surprise at all. Nevertheless, it required a response. Evans called in a team from the Anti-Terrorist Squad to perform further security checks and to remain on alert throughout the conference.

The King, *Defender of Faith*, adopting the revised title from his predecessor, was in conversation with leading members of the establishment and other popular and representative figures. They were meeting at Sandringham. It was unusual for the Royal Family to receive guests here as it was typically a place to which they retired during holidays for a little R&R. This meeting, however, was an interfaith discussion, striving for unity amongst the different religions. In attendance were the Archbishops of the Church of England, the Chief Rabbi, The Catholic Primate of All England, as well as representatives from the UK's Muslim, Hindu, Baha'i, Buddhist and other religious communities. Humanist and Atheist organisations were also represented. Others in attendance included university vice-chancellors and certain popular celebrities – soap-stars and footballers, and the like.

Katrina Al-Kadassa was making arrangements. She had a job to do. Fifty percent of her commission had already been transferred to her offshore account; the rest would follow on completion. This financing might have rendered her quest for the inheritance all but academic – in purely financial terms that is. But it was no longer about the money and never really had been. Katrina knew this, deep down, though she was not prone to extensive self-analysis. She simply decided what she wanted and went out and got it. No belief system – religious or political – had ever seduced her. Perhaps the nearest thing she had to a philosophical position was that proposed by Nietzsche, to espouse and become *Übermensch*.

⁓

Ironically, it was now more than ten years since a leading Islamic cleric had issued a *fatwa* against suicide bombers, declaring them unbelievers. More recently a former government minister had warned against branding all god-fearing Muslims as 'Islamists'. But tensions were continuing to rise and, just as there was an urban versus rural dimension to this, so too there were religious and political axes. Such issues were germane to the discussions underway at Sandringham. But solutions were hard to come by. An understanding that unity amongst delegates would not necessarily – would almost definitely not – mean agreement on all matters, was widely understood. But they needed to reach a consensus.

⁓

The meeting at Chequers was not going well. Radical policies seemed to have been less effective than hoped or intended. Options for action were dwindling and the outflow of funds from the City was reaching unacceptable levels. The withdrawal of HSBC, finally, from the UK had set a wave in motion that was likely to prove unstoppable. Unless the government were able to reassure the world that it could remain its financial capital, the country was finished. It would take a new Marshall Plan to bring it back from the abyss following such a collapse. But Anthony Miller was by no means finished; he merely accepted the situation as an opportunity to excel. At the forthcoming summit he planned to renegotiate existing links with the continental powers and to inform them that the UK borders would once again be enforced and expulsions of illegal immigrants would continue apace. Other domestic, issues would be dealt with internally, with recourse to armed troops if necessary.

BBC's Chief Political Editor, reporting from Chequers:

"Nothing is certain in politics but its unpredictability and its ruthlessness. That may still be true but today the Prime Minister has declared a 'no turning back' policy for his government, and the UK as a nation, in the face of demands for concessions from our European allies. How this negotiating stance will hold up at next week's European Summit remains to be seen."

~

Katrina Al-Kadassa continued making arrangements. There was much to do. She knew about the conference at Sandringham. She knew who would be in attendance. Dorothy would be arriving in a few days – just in time to take the rap, if all went according to plan. She savoured the thought of her scheme working like clockwork and congratulated herself on her own cleverness.

She seemed oblivious to questions of morality that arise in, and govern, most relationships. Whether this was a consciously adopted philosophical position, or merely a blind spot, it was difficult to tell. But, in the end, it made no difference. She had never been in love – infatuated, foolish, passionate, yes – but never in love. She simply made use of people to meet her own ends. She did this as naturally as breathing. But she was soon to discover how little she really knew about herself.

When Katrina walked by the pool later that evening she found a pair of sunglasses on a table. It was the table the writer had been sitting and working at all morning. An opportunity presented itself. She would return them to him tomorrow. As she stood by the pool she saw the swallows skimming over the water and gathering insects on the wing. Then, when the light had almost faded to darkness, a larger bird arced low over the pool. At first she thought it looked like an owl but then realised it must be a nightjar, just like the ones she had seen near Oxford, in the forest clearing where the tall pines and larches had been felled. She remembered the deep churring sound they made at dusk as she sat beneath a large oak on the edge of the clearing. And then it was dark and she turned back towards the hotel.

The next day she found the writer at his table as usual. She approached him directly.

"Excuse me," she said, "I found these by the pool last night. I thought they might be yours?"

He looked up from his laptop and looked at her and the sunglasses and smiled. Then he spoke:

"Well, thank you very much. I hadn't noticed they were missing. Very kind of you."

She smiled and turned and walked round to the far side of the pool to take up her place among the sunbathers. She felt her face redden but he could not see that. When she looked up about half an hour later he was no longer at his table. She could hear laughter coming from the nearby tennis courts; her playing partner was having a lesson with the hotel Pro. She picked up her book – throwaway reading by a verbose American writer about a contemporary quest for the Holy Grail – but she could not concentrate. Her plans were in place and all the elements were in order, but still she could not concentrate. She struggled to find some cause for this unnecessary agitation but could find none. She got up and plunged into the pool, hoping it would dispel her restlessness, and for a moment it did, as she swam underwater half the length of the pool before surfacing and drawing in a lungful of welcome air.

Her sleep was fitful that night. She adjusted the A/C but could not get comfortable – her mind was racing and her legs twitched. She got cramp in her foot and leapt out of bed in the middle of the night to walk it off and rid herself of the excruciating pain. When she did eventually fall asleep she was disturbed by strange dreams that might even have been nightmares. In one dream Dorothy was swimming in the sea and being dragged further from the shore by invisible tides until she was just a dot in the ocean; Katerina stood on the shore watching with disinterested curiosity. In another she was watching a bride in her white wedding gown standing by a newly dug grave. Then an older man led her away to a waiting car that somehow became an ocean-going motor launch, complete with its own captain and crew and an onboard swimming pool. She recognised the man but could not put a name to the face. When she woke in the morning she felt as if she still needed a good night's sleep. It was seven-thirty and she decided to get up and take a shower – there was no point just lying there with her mind still racing.

~

It was early afternoon and, after a light salad for lunch, she was once again lying on a lounger by the pool. It was mid-afternoon. She realised she needed more sun cream. As she pulled the bottle out of her bag, after a thorough rummage, she heard a voice say:

"Excuse me."

She looked up and it was the writer whom she had been studying with such fascination and whom she had spoken to yesterday.

"I'm John, John Lester. I'm a writer."

She was, just for a split second, surprised. Then she said:

"Yes, I know. I've been watching you – I mean I noticed you working." She felt clumsy and looked away.

"Do you need some help with the sun cream?"

"Why thank you, that's very kind of you. It's my shoulders and back I can't reach very easily." She had no idea why she had just said that.

She stood up and they shook hands with an awkward formality.

"My name's Katrina, by the way." She felt a bit dizzy.

Then she lay down again, on her front, and John carefully applied the suntan lotion. She felt his hands on her skin and it made her tingle.

"Would you like a drink?" he asked.

"Yes. I'll have a sangria, please."

He called the waiter over and ordered two cool sangrias.

They sipped slowly at the refreshing fizzy red liquid. An older couple were swimming in the pool but most people were still at their siesta. A cooling breeze blew gently from the west and a brightly coloured butterfly landed nearby on a small bush covered in purple flowers. After they had finished their drinks they agreed to meet later for dinner. He booked a restaurant in town for seven o'clock; they both preferred to eat early rather than late. She felt nervous and flushed, like a schoolgirl preparing for her prom.

Dinner was sophisticated, just as she had expected. She was not intimidated by the haute cuisine nor the ostentatious service. She was rather enjoying herself. Their conversation was interesting, without any intrusive subtext, and they seemed to genuinely enjoy each other's company. For Katrina this was altogether a new experience and she felt disorientated, slightly intoxicated even, though she had only had a single glass of white wine. He was charming, quite literally.

When they arrived back at the hotel she invited him in for a nightcap. Both of them knew this was a decision they would never be able to undo. It did not matter. There was only this moment and they were happy to share their loneliness together. It was not a sad thing between them. In the morning they still laughed, without regret, and ate a hearty breakfast together, brought by room service. Neither felt tainted or condemned.

∼

Erasmus would be arriving in Geneva on Sunday afternoon and John decided to go and meet him. He prepared a large name card that he could hold above his head as the arrivals exited immigration and cleared customs. He would be his chauffeur, driving the hotel courtesy car.

∼

The Sandringham Conference was almost at the end of its third and final day. Evans would be flying out to Geneva the next day, Monday.

As it happened Dorothy had a provisional booking on the same flight – she had thought to surprise Katrina by arriving a day early. As luck would have it – Sod's Law – she had a sore throat and a temperature. She realised she would not be able to travel that day. She rang the airline to change her flight.

~

On Wednesday Anthony Miller PM flew directly from Northholt military airbase, accompanied by his spouse. Whilst the PM was involved in serious discussions, with the UK's European allies, his partner Jules would be enjoying shopping in chic and expensive boutiques.

Geneva has a history of great historical importance. During the Renaissance it was a centre of learning. Calvin's Bible was printed there in the new 'Protestant Rome'. One of its most famous adopted sons was, of course, Voltaire, sage of the Enlightenment. Another was Rousseau, that colossus of political thinking and exhibitor par excellence of amour proper. Today it houses the United Nations High Commissioner for Human Rights, the United Nations High Commissioner for Refugees, the World Health Organization, and a plethora of other worthy international organisations. It is home to a cosmopolitan population whose citizens are drawn from all over the world, not merely Europe. Some would say Geneva is a microcosm of idealism in action and a harbour for administration, negotiation, and prevarication – all symptoms of organisations that have grown too big, too quickly, to be able to act promptly and decisively, however well-intentioned.

Anthony Miller, Prime Minister of the United Kingdom, was greeted with all due pomp and ceremony, as befits the leader of a major nation. He savoured the occasion and felt his confidence rise with an additional and unnecessary boost. The limousine was waiting beyond the line of assembled dignitaries and security staff and he did not rush to reach it. He especially liked inspecting the guard of honour and hearing the military band.

~

It was ten-thirty on Friday morning and Katrina was in position. She had good visibility across the entire area. Dorothy should be in place by now. She watched a small plane circle above and then land. Probably a celebrity, she thought, someone brought in specially to entertain the guests that evening. Katrina dialled a number from a burner phone, routing the call via a Russian ISP's server address. The drone arrived without warning and plummeted directly at its target, homing in on a young woman dressed in black.

~

#bbcbreakingnews

"PM assassinated in bomb attack at Geneva Summit"

Reggie was ready. Never mind constitutional niceties! He called the Palace. On a temporary basis only, it should be understood, the King agreed to act as Leader of a government of National Unity - the country needed strong and popular leadership.

The casualties of war were unfortunate but necessary. The PM's Chief of Security was among them. He would make sure the widow received her full pension entitlement, without any administrative delay. He contacted Johnson and withdrew him from Geneva. He would head up security for the King. He sent a message to Austin at GCHQ suggesting golf at his club on Saturday. He sent a bunch of flowers to Ms Jenkins, the PA he had inherited from Lionel upon his demise. Then he sat back in his chair, looking over the Thames, and poured himself a small celebratory drink from a half-size bottle hidden away at the back of the third drawer in his large mahogany desk. The proper order was now restored. Reggie had, at last, made his mark.

56. King

For one awful moment the President thought he would have to cancel his trip to the UK The thought of losing out on an opportunity to play golf on Scotland's hallowed ground was only outweighed by his wife's fear that she would not be able to go shopping in London. But they need not have worried.

The King was a very nice man, well mannered, not at all stuck up, and really quite friendly. He made them feel at ease immediately. He was amused by their mutual cultural differences and interested in idiomatic linguistic expressions. He was both knowledgeable and modest – a rare combination in an important man. He insisted that the President and his wife continue with their planned trip. They should not let the terrorists win. Besides, he wanted to ask the President's advice on certain affairs of state and, specifically, how to run the UK as if he were a president himself, in his one, and only one, intended term of office.

Zeb was delighted when he was asked to play not only at St Andrews but also at Wentworth which was, of course, virtually in His Majesty's back garden. Could he stay on an extra couple of days? Could he – heck he could! Robin had to work overtime to square things back home but hey, the President is the President, and what he says goes.

Meanwhile, King Arthur II, as he was affectionately known, realised that he himself was, essentially, only a figurehead, a symbol. He was needed to unite the nation in these troubled times. He had no intention of assuming any real political power but was acutely aware that, behind the scenes, others would be attempting to manipulate things to their own advantage.

Zeb was very helpful and gave freely of his experience and expertise in politics. He very much believed that you were measured not only by what you achieved, but also how you went about achieving it; it was a question of doing the right thing in the right way *and* getting it done. It wasn't easy but it was more successful in the longer run. He assured his new friend that this was how things worked; the King was grateful and told him so at a splendid banquet held at Balmoral Castle in the Scottish Highlands.

The Chief Rabbi had also given freely of his understanding of important matters, along with the Archbishop of Canterbury – but their contribution was more in the nature of moral guidance; it was in practical matters that the President of the U.S. of A. proved an incredibly useful and surprisingly reliable ally. The crash course in practical politics would stand His Majesty in good stead in the forthcoming negotiations with the UK's European allies. Furthermore, the USA was able to offer certain (unspecified) assistance and incentives to these negotiations.

If the position of leader or ruler is essentially one of lofty loneliness, then these two men were able to provide each other with some degree of solace. The King was now a widower and had no private comfort, except for his children, and the discovery of a new friend cheered him greatly. For his part the President was delighted to make a new friend, who came with no political baggage or angle on things, as any of his countrymen might have.

But they both knew that they would not be able to maintain their friendship easily. Duty would call, both State and Family, and they were not free agents. Nevertheless they promised each other, and themselves, that they would do all they could to stay in touch and meet up as often as possible. In fact a state visit to the USA was organised for the following spring. This would greatly enhance the President's chances of re-election that year, given the royalty-worship so many American citizens seemed to indulge in. It was curious that a nation without a royal family seemed to yearn for one – or at least the romance of one – whilst the nation with a Royal Family seemed to take them for granted or even disdain them.

His Majesty knew that, whilst groomed for theatrical displays and appearances, he had no real political power or understanding. After much advice he realised that he was merely in the service of the people he led, as he had always been. He was prepared to accept his duty and his destiny, as his family before him had always done. He understood that, through his sacrifice, others would be able to live their lives in peace. That would have to be enough - he at least had a purpose.

57. Geneva

Katrina had no idea that Erasmus would be arriving that day. She had planned to return to the UK as soon as possible, to deal with unfinished business there. Now that she had completed her commission, and as soon as the rest of the fee was paid into her account, she could draw a line under this operation. She mourned her lapdog for a moment, but Dorothy would be missed only as a persistent itch is missed when it finally subsides. Katrina had no time for sentimentality. She had only just started to begin to learn what feeling for another person might be like and, so far, she had not realised exactly what it was she had recently experienced.

~

John arrived at the airport in good time to collect Erasmus. He had dressed the part of a chauffeur with a dark suit, tie and the obligatory peaked cap. He felt quite the part behind his dark glasses.

Erasmus' flight was delayed by almost thirty minutes. John had time to get a coffee while he was waiting. He was on 'airport time' – a slowing down of time common to all airports and endured by all frequent and infrequent, first and last time, flyers. It is surpassed in its seemingly interminable duration only by 'hospital time', where things move even more slowly. Nowadays he only felt an occasional twinge in his left leg, especially when the weather changed. Eventually passengers started to exit the doors into the arrivals hallway. John held the name card aloft. Of course, he recognised Erasmus immediately, though he was shorter than he had envisaged. Erasmus spotted his name and approached John, hauling his single suitcase behind him.

"Welcome to Geneva, Inspector Erasmus," said the chauffeur.

"Thank you. Glad to be here," replied Erasmus.

They walked over to the parking area, John taking his luggage, and stopped at a dark blue Mercedes saloon. John put the suitcase in the boot of the car and opened the rear passenger door for his client. They had to stop at a police checkpoint on leaving the airport – security was at red alert following the previous day's terrorist outrage – their route took them away from the centre of town, along the E62 and then back towards the city along the north-western shore of *Lac Leman*.

"So this is your first time in Switzerland Inspector?"

"Yes, it is."

"It is a holiday, perhaps?"

"No, I'm afraid not. Most definitely business."

John, asked no more but concentrated on his driving and thought about what might happen later that evening. He was still not sure.

∼

Katrina was looking forward to dinner in the evening. John had invited her to dine with him at the hotel. He said he would be bringing an old friend with him, whom he would like her to meet. She was intrigued but John would give no clues as to his friend's identity. All would be revealed soon enough. She was excited, but tried not to show it. Most of all she was confident. No one had ever paid her such attention before, not even her father, and certainly no one as worldly and sophisticated as John. She felt almost flattered.

She decided, on impulse and surprising herself, to make a booking at a beauty parlour downtown. Short notice was not a problem to this high-grade establishment that catered especially for the rich, and money was no object to Katrina. She wanted to look and feel her best; she didn't want to disappoint John or let herself down.

While she was waiting for the hour to arrive she took a stroll on the veranda, overlooking the hotel gardens. A colourful small bird was preening and washing itself in a stone basin held aloft by the goddess Aphrodite.

Its bright feathers glistened in the sun as it flapped and splashed. Suddenly a hawk darted out of the hedge and plucked the tiny creature from its perch; death came swiftly and silently. A shiver ran down her spine and she turned and walked quickly back to the hotel lobby.

∼

When Erasmus checked in to the hotel he had a message waiting for him. He was invited to dinner that evening, at a nearby restaurant, by a Mr John Crossland. This name was unfamiliar to him but he was no longer on his own territory and must assume this was part of the Author's well-designed plot.

"May I leave a message for Mr Crossland please?" he asked the desk clerk. "Tell him I will be pleased to join him for dinner this evening."

∼

Dinner was a little later this evening, at eight o'clock. Katrina had agreed to meet John for drinks by the pool at seven-thirty. It was only seven o'clock now and she was ready but she mustn't appear too early, or seem too keen. A quarter to eight would be about right – no later. Till then she must distract herself.

∼

Of the three, only John knew that they would be meeting together for the first time tonight. He wanted things to go well. His protagonist and his antagonist, seated together at the same table. What a timeless tableau they would form, the three of them, revealed in a particular moment, painted for eternity in the mind of the Reader. John had not felt this nervous and excited for a long time, if ever. He could not remember anything like it. This was new, this was something special. He felt proud and helpless, like a father holding his firstborn. He needed to steady himself before he began the difficult traverse across the rock face that seemed to present itself immediately in front of him. The story had taken over and he was merely another character in its demesne.

~

At seven-thirty precisely Erasmus arrived by pre-booked taxi at the restaurant. Waiting for him was an elegantly dressed man, perhaps in his late forties or early fifties, whom he immediately recognised as the chauffeur who had collected him from the airport earlier that day. He gave a wry smile.

"I am sorry to have played that little trick on you," John said, "but I was curious to meet you without prejudice. I hope you don't mind?"

"Not at all," replied Erasmus, "I would probably have done the same myself."

"It is good to meet you at last," said John.

"And you too," said Erasmus - "What now, I wonder?"

"Indeed. A drink perhaps?"

"Just a tomato juice please, with ice."

"Yes, of course, on duty. I shall have a Martini."

He called the waiter over and ordered their drinks.

"I hope you don't mind," said John, "but I've invited a young lady to join us for dinner. I think you may know her, though I am not sure you have actually met."

"Oh, I see. I'm sure that's no problem," Erasmus replied.

Katrina made her entrance. She was stunning. Her hair was waved in an immaculate forties style – something she had learnt from Harriet – and her dress was a beautiful shimmering turquoise, with deft darts and pleats that accentuated her lithe figure. John was delighted but Erasmus was surprised and shocked, though he wasn't clear why. He knew instantly who she was. The fact that he had been expecting to meet her did nothing to diminish his sense of danger and bewilderment, as if they had reached the top of a mountain where they all now stood perched together on a sharp and perilous *arête*.

Previously so sure of himself, and the fitness of his plan, Erasmus now found himself at a loss – for words, for ideas, for action. It was as if he had been winded by an unexpected blow to the solar plexus.

John was the first to react: "You look absolutely beautiful, my dear!" And he gave her a peck on the cheek. Katrina realised this was as she should expect in company, no more.

"Let me introduce you to Inspector Julian Erasmus, a long-time acquaintance and, dare I say, friend of mine."

Katrina holds out her hand and Erasmus takes it firmly and shakes it as he looks at her, unblinking. She looks at him and does not avert her gaze.

John feels immensely pleased: he has succeeded in bringing together his two protégés, the two characters of whom he is most proud.

And then they are called to table and John offers her his arm; Erasmus follows them and they walk out onto the veranda, where they are seated, by an immaculately dressed and discrete maitre d', at a table beside the balcony.

The incongruity of this formality and politeness grates with Erasmus at a visceral level; it somehow offends his innate sense of justice, or perhaps it is just his non-conformist heritage that objects.

They review the menu and make their selections for *hors d'oeuvre* and a main course. John selects a fine Bavarian white wine; they are happy to defer to his specialist knowledge in this field.

Katrina is revelling in the obvious discomfort Erasmus feels in her presence, and the close attention she induces in John.

Their conversation is initially stilted, then becomes more than superficially exploratory, probing for weakness and searching for any chinks in each other's armour. John observes this exchange between two brilliant minds, between two people who are so strong in their own identities and sense of being. They finish the entrees and there is a short delay before the next course arrives.

∼

It is quarter to eight and Pabin is in position. She has good visibility across the entire area. They will be in place soon. She watches a small plane fly over towards Cointrin, Geneva's International Airport. Now she waits and watches as the guests come out onto the veranda for dinner.

~

Erasmus spoke next:

"You know, of course, that I came in search of you both – for different reasons but with an equal degree of justification?" Both John and Katrina nodded.

"And *I* came here to wait for *you*, Inspector," said Katrina. "But oddly enough I also found John, though I wasn't looking for him, but it seems we have, each in our own way, discovered him!"

John smiled, and he blushed – he could not help it.

The main course was served. The waiter moved quietly away from the table and, as Katrina looked across to John, he noticed a faint red dot in the middle of her forehead, like a Hindu woman might wear at the Festival of Diwali, only this was not painted onto the surface of her skin but seemed to be a small circle of light. A look of horror came across his face and Katrina leant forward slightly with a seemingly puzzled look. Then she slumped back in her chair. A small trickle of bright red blood began to run, like a tiny rivulet, from a small hole in her left temple. She was dead.

Erasmus looked at Katrina Al-Kadassa for just a moment, then turned to look at John.

"I didn't know, I didn't know!" he exclaimed.

And then it dawned on Erasmus: it was true that John didn't know – couldn't possibly have known – that this was going to happen. How could he?

58. Letter from The Author

Dear Reader,

I suppose you have realised this, or at least suspected it. I can now confirm it is so. John went to such lengths that one might have assumed he must be the Author – but he was, in fact, merely another character in the story. My 'character'. But now the I will speak for myself, directly, and you will have the opportunity to judge for yourself what I have to say:

"It is finished. The sound of cicadas rattles the dry air, and dust plumes up from my sandals in small clouds, as I walk along the track to the farm. A large black bumble bee inspects a pale yellow flower and a bright green lizard darts into a crack in the dry stone wall as I pass. Rough chippings and red earth form this track; it is lined with dark cypresses trees. They are well suited to coping with the heat and offer a little shade, giving up their sweet scent as I brush past them. It is early afternoon, siesta time, when the Tuscan sun is at its hottest. I am enjoying some time alone and I wander along slowly, not rushing to get from A to B. I reflect that I have not always enjoyed my own company; it has taken me many years to appreciate its worth. Perhaps I will have a swim in the pool later."

~

Of course this is not the case. I am not in Italy this summer. Nor am I lying on a beach in the south of Spain. Nor am I sitting alone in a busy London Park among long-deprived sun-worshippers who have stripped to the waist and are starting to resemble a pod of boiled lobsters. In fact I am not holidaying at all. This month I have been working at my

206

desk, or in my favourite armchair, writing a thriller of sorts. The cat (that I do not have) has been trying to interrupt me and insinuate itself into my work, interrupting my concentration and insisting on being fed. If you will excuse me for a moment, while I find its dinner in one of these cupboards?

~

Now where were we? Ah yes: You may have picked up my book when browsing for something to read, perhaps as you were waiting at the airport for a connecting flight to Geneva or Nairobi? Or it may have been given to you as a present, or recommended by a friend who has kindly lent it to you? Perhaps Jennifer sent you an early copy for review? Of course, I do not know; I cannot know.

You are sure of your own role in this affair, I presume? You are the Reader. Without you there is no story. My role? Well, I have appeared in the story, of course, but I am neither Erasmus nor John, nor any other of the several characters who appear. However, if I were to say that, nevertheless, I do exist, what would that mean?

I am not, alas, on holiday in Italy. Even if I were somewhere sitting in the sun or standing in the rain, it would hardly matter. What is certain is that we, that is to say you and I, have now finished this story. Or so I believe.